THE COCKFIGHT

THE COCKFIGHT

For Dave

Frank Abrams

Frank Abrams
3/16/25

PUBLISHED BY FRANK ABRAMS

©Frank Abrams, 2023

Contact information: abramstra@gmail.com

https://www.facebook.com/frankabramsauthor/

ISBN 979-8-9910735-0-9 (for Softcover Version).

ISBN 979-8-9910735-1-6 (for eBook)

Original Cover Design © Frank Abrams

Without limiting the rights under copyright reserved above, no part of this publication may be reproduced, stored in or introduced in a retrieval system, or transmitted, in any form, or by any means (electronic, mechanical, recording, photocopying, or otherwise) without the prior written permission of both the copyright owner/publisher of the book

Disclaimer: This is a work of fiction. Unless otherwise indicated, all the names, characters, businesses, places, events and incidents in this book are either the product of the author's imagination or used in a fictitious manner. Any resemblance to actual persons, living or dead, or actual events is purely coincidental.

PREFACE

THE COCKFIGHT is a story about injustice and redemption. Although it is fiction, many of the facts concerning the law and its application are or were authentic at the time the story is set, and are still factual.

The sad part is that in many situations there is or has been little remedy for the wrongs that have been perpetrated against innocent people. We live in a society that is quick to judge but slow to recognize the fact that individuals are presumed to be innocent, and that the burden is entirely on the government to prove guilt. Further, there is little or no accountability or acceptance of responsibility when things go wrong.

We live in an imperfect world where ideas and ideals relating to "justice," are merely aims that are rarely reached. In the so called "Land of the Free," America's prisons are filled with more people per capita than virtually any other country. The American prison population has grown five hundred percent in the last forty years, and the operative assumption is that once charged, always guilty.

What's even worse is that we continue to punish offenders even after they are released. With felony records, they cannot obtain meaningful work or be allowed to become productive members of society. Once placed on such lists as the "Sex offender registry," a person's productive life is in essence over, even if that placement was in error.

I wrote THE COCKFIGHT to illustrate what can happen when things go wrong. My hope is that this book will lead to a change in both attitude and action, that injustice will no longer be tolerated

FRANK ABRAMS

*This book is dedicated to
all individuals who have suffered
injustice under color of law*

TABLE OF CONTENTS

CHAPTER ONE: Welcome To Hell 1

CHAPTER TWO: A Better Place 5

CHAPTER THREE: The Morning Meal 7

CHAPTER FOUR: Varumpt Varumpt Varumpt 11

CHAPTER FIVE: Teacher Of The Year 15

CHAPTER SIX: The Oldest Spectator Sport 21

CHAPTER SEVEN: Dinner 25

CHAPTER EIGHT: The Grand Event 31

CHAPTER NINE: A Small Side Trip 37

CHAPTER TEN: No Reservations Required 41

CHAPTER ELEVEN: An Apparition 45

CHAPTER TWELVE: Enhancing Human Existence 49

CHAPTER THIRTEEN: The American Dream 53

CHAPTER FOURTEEN: A Modern American Business Model 55

CHAPTER FIFTEEN: The Trip Back 59

CHAPTER SIXTEEN: All Saints Church Of The Holy Deliverer 63

CHAPTER SEVENTEEN: Anxious For Breakfast 67

CHAPTER EIGHTEEN: Varumpt Varumpt Varumpt Screech 71

CHAPTER NINETEEN: A Real American Hero 75
CHAPTER TWENTY: One Fine Rooster 81
CHAPTER TWENTY-ONE: Prayers Answered................................ 85
CHAPTER TWENTY-TWO: Lord's Mercy...................................... 89
CHAPTER TWENTY-THREE: Ten Stories of Hell............................ 93
CHAPTER TWENTY-FOUR: A Systematic Training Program........... 97
CHAPTER TWENTY-FIVE: The Long Walk Back........................... 103
CHAPTER TWENTY-SIX: Feeling Low.. 107
CHAPTER TWENTY-SEVEN: An Offer You Cannot Refuse 111
CHAPTER TWENTY-EIGHT: Research.. 113
CHAPTER TWENTY-NINE: Continuing Criminal Enterprise......... 117
CHAPTER THIRTY: Tomorrow Night.. 121
CHAPTER THIRTY-ONE: No- one Here By That Name 125
CHAPTER THIRTY-TWO: The Letter 129
CHAPTER THIRTY-THREE: The Philosophy Of Vagrancy 133
CHAPTER THIRTY-FOUR: I'd Rather Be Fishing 137
CHAPTER THIRTY-FIVE: Let's Get Out of Here............................ 141
CHAPTER THIRTY-SIX: Thirty Days To Fitness 145
CHAPTER THIRTY-SEVEN: Cat Scratch Fever 149
CHAPTER THIRTY-EIGHT: A Stranger 153
CHAPTER THIRTY-NINE: Descended From Monkeys 157
CHAPTER FORTY: Bad News 161
CHAPTER FORTY-ONE: The Letter For Reconsideration................ 165
CHAPTER FORTY-TWO: A Day In The Sun.................................. 169
CHAPTER FORTY-THREE: The Shanghai Rooster......................... 173

CHAPTER FORTY-FOUR: Fight Night 175

CHAPTER FORTY-FIVE: The Long Row To Hoe 177

CHAPTER FORTY-SIX: Notice of Hearing... 181

CHAPTER FORTY-SEVEN: Back From The Dead 185

CHAPTER FORTY-EIGHT: The Big Day Coming 189

CHAPTER FORTY-NINE: The Hearing 193

CHAPTER FIFTY: It Gets Worse... 197

CHAPTER FIFTY-ONE: Day Two 203

CHAPTER FIFTY-TWO: The Ruling... 215

CHAPTER FIFTY-THREE: A Surprise.. 217

CHAPTER FIFTY-FOUR: The Most Hated Inmates 225

CHAPTER FIFTY-FIVE: The Decision.. 229

CHAPTER FIFTY-SIX: The Gift... 233

CHAPTER FIFTY-SEVEN: The Equation of Injustice...................... 237

CHAPTER FIFTY-EIGHT: News From The Government 239

CHAPTER FIFTY-NINE: A Funeral And A Wedding 241

CHAPTER SIXTY: The Dade County Youth & Agricultural Fair..........243

Chapter One:
Welcome To Hell

The gleaming stiletto knife was hard to miss, even in the dim light emanating from the causeway streetlights above, as the red blood that covered the wooden handle dripped from the hand of the man who was viciously plunging the knife, over and over again, into the stomach of a tattoo covered recipient.

The tattoo covered victim of the blows doubled over as the knife sliced through his stomach one last time, the blade appearing again as it exited his back. As the mortally wounded man slowly sunk to the ground, the assailant let go of the sharp and angry looking implement.

"He tried to rape me, he tried to rape me! Die you bastard, Die! You had it coming," he said pleadingly as he turned toward the several grubby and dirty looking men who came running over.

The last of these men, dressed in clerical garb, had a noticeable limp. With the aid of a barely functional prosthetic leg, he hobbled toward the affray. "Is he dead, Ebenezer?" asked the man with the prosthetic leg, his lyrical Irish accent clear and unmistakable.

"He's more than dead, he's cut up like a jigsaw puzzle."

"He tried to rape me, I had to defend myself, I had to," the assailant tearfully repeated as he sat down, head in hands.

"Now there, there, son," calmingly said the man in clerical garb, "you did what you had to do."

"I can't go to jail, I'll die there, I'll die."

"Teach, what do you think we should do?" asked Ebenezer," a lithe, dirty and heavily bearded man who had run with the others to investigate the affray.

"I'll defer to Preach on this one."

Four or five men, Teach and Preach included, gathered together and quietly began to discuss the situation.

"We've got a dead man here," said Teach, "we can't alert the authorities, if they come, they'll just throw everyone in jail."

"Preach?"

"Well, for one thing, I think that we need to give the gentleman a decent burial, don't you?" All present nodded their heads.

"And I think he should be assisted to the briny bottom with a few hundred pounds of rock tied to his arms and legs," said Ebenezer.

"You better remove those appendages," replied another man, "or they'll figure out who he is. We can use that knife there to cut off his arms, legs, and head." Several men worked fast as they butchered the body, they affixed heavy boulders and tied them to the torso of the dead man. Next they put the arms, legs and head in a heavy duty trash bag, and weighted it down as well.

Holding a weathered and stained King James Bible, Preach began to read aloud; "I speak after the manner of men because of the infirmity of your flesh, for as ye have yielded your members servants to uncleanliness and to iniquity, unto iniquity even so now, yield your members servants to righteousness unto holiness."

"The wages of sin are death, but the gift of God is eternal life through Jesus Christ our Lord."

"Ashes to ashes, dust to dust, we now commit the dead to his final resting place. We hereby commit this humble sex offender to the sea." With that the men holding the deceased man's remains looked over at Preach. Preach nodded his head and with a heave ho, they threw the dead man's torso into the dark waters of the bay, followed next by the bag holding his arms, legs and head.

After the improvised funeral, Preach made his way to where Teach was standing. "No one asked what you were thinking about," he quietly said.

"I'll tell you what I'm thinking about, I'm thinking of getting as far away from this place as I can. I'm leaving this God Damn sex offender colony, this Julia Tuttle place, a place that they named after the founder of Miami and which represents all that injustice can measure. This is Hell, Preach, and I'm leaving."

"Hell? Hell, you say?" "This isn't Hell, just a bump in the road."

"I don't care what you say, Preach, I'm getting out of here."

"Before you leave, I've been thinking about the same. There may well be a better place."

"Like Heaven?" he chuckled.

"No, my friend, although Heaven is preferable, I'm talking about the General Douglas MacArthur Causeway. I've a friend named Amos who could use some good strong arms and legs, fate has placed him in a wheelchair and I think that you could be of assistance. Those folks over there could use some spiritual guidance as well."

Chapter Two:

A Better Place

The ragged looking black man in the wheelchair screamed loudly as the two roosters fought it out in the pit. "Come on, Come on, Tear him up, Tear him up!" Both roosters launched at each other, legs kicking, feathers flying.

The pit was a twenty by twenty-foot hole, dug two feet deep into the sand that lay underneath a large cement causeway. Over a hundred and fifty men were gathered around to watch the events that were unfolding underneath. Bright lights illuminated the darkness of the night as the bridge dwellers, those who actually lived under the bridge, and the many others who came to promote and watch the cockfights, gathered in the sand around the pit.

There was a separate area with a scale, where the roosters would be weighed before they were placed in the fighting hole with their opponent. A man would walk around taking note of bets and collecting money.

Bettors would raise their hands, fingers denoting the amount, in hundreds of dollars that they would place on the rooster they had a hunch on, birds that had sharp spikes attached to their legs with leather bands. These spikes, called "knives," multiplied the effectiveness of the swift and deadly kicks that the fighting cocks thrust toward one another.

They were also dubbed. Dubbing is the act to trimming off their comb and wattle with a razor blade, the fleshy parts that stuck out from their head and hung low below their neck. They would do this to minimize blood loss during the cockfights.

The knives that are attached to the legs of fighting cocks make the fights particularly brutal. Although roosters have natural spurs that emanate from the side of their legs, the artificial appendages make the fights bloody and deadly, so deadly in fact that trainers of these birds have been killed, and in some rare cases, even spectators of these brutal animal contests.

Bloody, heartless and depraved are just a few of the descriptions that have been used to describe what transpires at these events, and the event that was taking place under the MacArthur Causeway that evening was no different.

A brown colored rooster was in the pit with his opponent, a black rooster of approximately the same size. They continuously jumped up toward each other, wings flapping, legs kicking, deadly knives attached.

The brown cock appeared to be winning as the black one seemed to lose energy. Blood was visible on its head, neck and beak.

"Come on come on, get up, get up!" yelled the black man in the wheelchair toward the mortally wounded rooster, but it was of no avail. The referee walked into the pit and lifted the winner into the air to show all gathered who the victor was. The black rooster lay dead on the floor of the pit. The crowd excitedly collected their winnings, or in this case, regretted their misplaced bets.

Chapter Three:

The Morning Meal

"You're playin with my mind, there's no conceivable way that a high-quality bird like that is walking the streets of Miami," said the black man from his wheelchair as Teach pushed the chair down Northeast Second Avenue in the middle of downtown Miami.

On their right hobbled Preach, always doing his best to keep up with his barely adequate but somehow functional prosthesis.

"The chance of encountering a Flarry Eyed Grey loose on the streets of Miami is about as improbable as finding a man on the moon."

"I'm telling you Amos, that that's what I heard," replied Teach, "Garcia heard it from Apache, who spoke to One Eye who heard it from No Brains."

"Well, there you go, the rumor started with No Brains."

"Hey look, you didn't listen to me last night," Teach responded, "and look where we're heading for breakfast."

With that the hobbling man in clerical garb spoke up, and with his clear and lyrical Irish accent said, "God always provides, look at the birds of the air who neither sow nor reap, God feeds them. Sometimes amazing things happen."

"Hey, I ain't looking for no bird of the air, just one good fighting rooster who stands his ground," all three of them laughed as they came in sight of the

Christian House of Charity where they would partake of their morning meal.

"I hope that they don't mix the food all together again today, it's bad enough to have to eat the slop they dish out without it being mixed with the old slop from before," said Teach, "it's worse than what we used to serve the kids in the public-school cafeterias."

"Beggars can't be choosers, be thankful for what you've got."

"That sure do make sense, Preach," responded the wheelchair bound man, "Me, I got two legs that don't work, you got one leg missing, and Teach, well I'm not sure what he's missing but he sure ain't like he was before."

"No, you're right," replied Teach," but I'll never give in to those bastards, they'll never have the privilege of watching me grovel in the dirt."

With those words they approached a long line of unkempt, unbathed and dirty smelling men, lined outside of a building with large words, "CHRISTIAN HOUSE OF CHARITY." A sign with the words, "NO CURSING, SWEARING, FIGHTING OR SPITTING ALLOWED," was affixed to the cafeteria entryway door.

As the line of two hundred men and a few women filed through, a lady behind the serving counter spoke directly to Amos as he sat in the wheelchair, "How you doing today, looks like you've got your buddies with you?"

"Yeah, they like my magnetic personality," his mouth opened to a wide smile, "Say, you ain't got no filet mignon today?" "No, just bean curd mixed with vegetables and scrambled egg."

"Go figure," said Teach, his face showing clear signs of resignation.

The man in clerical garb addressed the lady, "I'll have some of that wonderful bean curd with the mixed vegetables and scrambled egg." He then looked Teach and spoke the words, "Life is all about attitude, tis more important than anything else."

As they sat at the wooden table and began to eat, two men approached. One, a somewhat overweight and unclean man wearing a t-shirt with the words, "Little Big Horn Was Just The Beginning," along with him was a skinny man who had a vacant look in his eyes.

"Well here comes Apache and No Brains, you can ask them yourself."

"Rumor has it that you folks have encountered a high quality fightin cock walking the streets of Miami?"

"Not me," said the man with the pony tail, "No Brains over here spied it just yesterday."

With that, all four looked at No Brains for the story. His eyes began to dart around in different directions as he leaned forward and began speaking in a raspy squirrel like voice.

"I had come across a little extra cash from a nice lady driving an expensive car, so I put down my 'I Will Work For Food' sign, and headed over to the All Day And Night Convenience Store for a bottle of Mad Dog."

"I'd been drinking for ten or fifteen minutes when I heard a 'clucking' noise. I looked up and as I focused my eyes, I couldn't believe it."

"There, sitting just a few feet away, was the most spectacular creature God has ever devised. I'd encountered one years before at a cock fight in the Redlands, down in South Dade, I put all of my money on what turned out to be the meanest, angriest, and most ornery bird ever put on this earth."

"He ripped the other bird to shreds, it was not a pretty sight, but before I could collect my winnings, the cops arrived and busted up the gathering and I ran away as fast as I could. Funny thing, no-one was ever charged with anything, they just let us run away and took all of our money, never made a penny, the cops took all that," he slowly shook his head from side to side.

"Describe this bird for us," asked Amos.

"Well, nearest I can remember, she had a beautiful black chest and tail, her feathers the best I've ever seen. Her head, top and sides were covered with silky brownish white feathers and her beak and comb as red as the red lips of Marilyn Monroe.

"You know that a rooster is male and a hen is female," replied Teach.

"There he goes, let him finish his story, Mr. Know It All."

"What happened next?" asked Preach.

"Well, I tried calling him to come over, 'Here chicky chicky,' 'Here chicky chicky,' then I remembered that I had some sunflower seeds in my pocket. I threw a few toward him and as he came closer, I could see that he was a young and skinny rascal but still quite a specimen."

"I reached out to grab him, but he ran like Moses from the Egyptians." They all laughed.

Breakfast finished, Teach, Preach and Amos departed for their humble abode. As they walked back down Northeast 2nd Avenue, Teach leaned down to read the headlines visible through a newspaper vending machine.

One particular story caught his attention, "DNA LAB ERROR SENDS INNOCENT MAN TO JAIL"

"Hey, anyone got some change?" he asked as he unsuccessfully pulled on the door of the machine. Just then, someone walked by and deposited enough money to purchase a paper for himself, and Teach reached in and grabbed one for himself just before the door slammed shut.

Chapter Four:

VARUMPT! VARUMPT! VARUMPT!

The General Douglas MacArthur Causeway connects Downtown Miami with South Miami Beach. Named after America's last five star general and war hero, it is a busy and traffic laden six lane structure that for the most part runs east to Miami Beach and West to the mainland. Thousands of vehicles travel over the causeway every day, literally every type imaginable, from small compact cars to large freight moving interstate trucks.

Along the way it connects to affluent communities populated by the super wealthy, communities such as Palm, Star and Hibiscus Islands. Large mansions with expensive yachts parked in adjacent waters are seen to the north. The late Al Capone's own mansion was within a stone's throw from this well-traveled bridge.

To the South is the Port of Miami, where hundreds of thousands of tourists embark on exotic cruises to the Caribbean. Large luxury liners line the docks, awaiting their appointed time of debarkation.

Living under a bridge beneath a busy and traffic laden causeway is somewhat problematic and takes getting used to, for one thing, there is the incessant noise of fast cars and large trucks racing overhead, "Varumpt! Varumpt! Varumpt! Varumpt! Ceaseless and unending.

Secondly, you are living on a small spit of sand, exposed to the winds and the elements, on both sides. Other issues arise, such as restroom and bath facilities, there's no electricity, and food, unless canned, will spoil. Residents have gotten around those problems by defecating directly into the Bay, which is also where they take their baths. Drinking water is kept in bottles, and canned food is stored along with whatever possessions a resident may have.

Privacy is arranged through the placement of discarded cardboard boxes arranged into partitions, walls made of old smelly and rotten blankets or plastic tarp salvaged from the roadway. Poorly secured, and having departed from boats pulled on trailers, many times they will fly off into the wind.

But there's one thing that living under the Causeway provides that even the super wealthy on the surrounding islands cannot boast of, a better view. While the super wealthy look out of their back windows and see hordes of homeless men taking baths in the open and defecating into the bay, the residents of the bridge community have the pleasurable vista of gorgeous Mediterranean style mansions with nearby large and expensive yachts. To the South, they see megalithic cruise ships packed with happy tourists.

If the wind and rain isn't blowing in too hard from the north or south, the prospect of living under the Causeway can be described as Miami living at its best.

"Tis a wonderful day, isn't it," observed Preach as he relaxed on an old and dirty mattress that had stains and discoloration of all sorts. A mattress whose smell could best be described as a combination of rotten eggs and spoiled fish, only worse.

Next to his mattress lay a well-worn copy of The King James Bible. There were old and yellowed papers pushed into a file and one yellowed and almost illegible letter duct taped to the wall behind him, its faded words reading "Certificate Of Ordination To The Holy Priesthood."

Sitting nearby was Teach. He appeared engrossed in the article he was reading.

"You look like you're reading something serious," said Preach, as he sprayed a can of Lysol in the air and smacked a fly that landed on his cheek.

"Well," replied Teach, it's an article about DNA labs and screw-ups, you know that my case concerned similar lies. They talked about the one in a billion chance that the DNA collected came from someone else, then they used it to destroy my life.

"What exactly is DNA evidence?"

Teach looked at Preach with resignation as he slowly put down his newspaper, out fell an advertising flyer for "Fantastic Christmas Specials, 2009 Will Be Our Best Sale Ever."

"DNA is how the government screwed me, they used it to connect me to something that never happened."

Teach pulled an old notebook from under his sleeping bag, there was a collection of articles. He leafed through and pulled one out. It had a banner headline;

"TEACHER OF THE YEAR ARRESTED FOR RAPE OF STUDENT"

As he began to read, a few others stopped by to listen.

Ebenezer was a man in his early forties with greyish yellow hair and a long beard, he had spent most of his life in the outdoors, and his face, lined with wrinkles, skin burnt brown with reddish blotches, told the story.

One Lip sat to the left of Ebenezer. One lip was a man whose bottom lip had somehow been gnawed away by some pernicious disease or evil act, he had trouble speaking and often drooled and spit as he spoke.

Then there was Flathead, a man in his early twenties who wore military fatigues and sported a crewcut. No-one knew much about him, except that he drifted in from the mountains of North Carolina. His left upper armed showed a long horrible looking scar that looked as if someone from a butcher shop had whacked it a few places with a large meat cleaver and Dr. Frankenstein had sewn it back together. Once in a while, he would rub his arm as he winced in pain.

Amos in his wheelchair came round too, a man in his mid-forties, confined to a wheelchair for all of eternity, his face showing lines evidencing long years of struggle, a kind of sadness coupled with melancholy, and a kind of wisdom accumulated through years of hard times. They all gathered closer, as the whistling noise from the wind, and the incessant "Varumpt" "Varumpt" "Varumpt" of cars passing overhead, pervaded the air. Teach commenced reading the article out loud.

Chapter Five:

Teacher of The Year

"William Bradford, Teacher of the Year, has been arrested and charged with the vicious rape of one of his female students. Mr. Bradford, whom witnesses say was in the process of attempting intercourse with the unnamed female, who is a minor, was allegedly stopped in the act by two men who just happened to be passing by when they heard the screams of the young victim.

"Both witnesses say that the attack was brutal and that if they had not chanced upon the attack as it was happening, injuries to the victim might have been even more severe. The unnamed female is presently being treated at a local hospital near Brunswick Georgia where the attack occurred.

"Mr. Bradford is being held in secure confinement in the Glynn County Georgia jail. Glynn County is where Brunswick is located. At this time there is no bond."

"So, tell me what really happened," asked Ebenezer, "cause this sounds like a whole lot of crap."

"The only truth to the article was the part about me being an 'award winning teacher.'" "I used to teach math and science at Francis Langhorne Dade Middle School here in Miami. The parents and administrators used to say that

I really 'cared' for my students. They said that I 'went overboard,' and that they were 'thankful' to have a teacher such as myself."

"Didn't you have a wife and kids?" asked Preach

"Yeah, I was married and have a boy and a girl, at least I used to. When I'd arrive at home from a hard day of work, they'd run up and hug me. Before my wife changed, she thought that I was the light of her life, then they started foisting these lies against me, listen to this one," he picked up another yellowed article from his notebook and began to read the large print, 'ANOTHER EMBARASSMENT AS TEACHER ABUSES HIS TRUST.'"

"Listen to this shit, 'Another teacher has abused his position by using it to prey on young female students, until strong measures are taken against these individuals who take advantage of their position, these sewer scum will continue to cause incalculable harm and damage. They must be removed from the community for good, put in jail with the key thrown away, or the message will not get across.'"

"He called me 'sewer scum,' but the real scum is the guy who wrote this editorial."

"You can't look backward, you have to go forward," went Preach.

"Didn't you once say that telling a person's story is good for the soul, that it's 'cathartic,'" replied Ebenezer.

"I guess I did," replied Preach, "so why don't you tell us about your wife and family?"

"My wife and I met when we were undergraduates in college and we were very much in love."

"I came from humble beginnings and worked hard to get myself through, my hard work paid off as I received scholarships based upon my commitment and work ethic. I always wanted to be a teacher and felt it the finest career that anyone could aspire, to make a difference in a young person's life, what better endeavor could one attain to do?

"I received a great honor. In 1994 I was named 'Teacher of the Year,' not just in my school, but for the entire school system. There were parties held in my honor, I traveled to all of the county schools and gave well received speeches about the importance of caring about one's students. They all congratulated me. Little did I know that it would all come back one day to bite me in the ass."

"I know all about that 'ass biting' thing," replied Amos.

"Christmas of 1995 was going to be special, because of the fine job we had done as teachers, indicated by the many accomplishments of our students, they arranged for us to take a trip to the Smithsonian Institution in Washington DC.

"It was to be a one-week trip, and three classes were crowded onto two school buses. We had planned the trip well in advance, and there were to be two chaperones on each bus. I was assigned to bus number two along with Ms. White, another math and science teacher, but come the day of the trip, she contracts some kind of virus and can't travel. Without another chaperone to be found, it was either me alone in Bus Two or no trip at all."

"I kissed my wife goodbye and hugged my children. I didn't know that it would be the last time that I would ever have any real contact with them again."

One Lip listened intently as a spittle of drool dripped to his shirt.

"I boarded the bus with twenty-seven restless and rambunctious fourteen-year-old kids, incessant noise, screaming, laughing and hollering. The bus left the school parking lot and commenced its trip northward.

"I sat in the back of the bus, in order to have a better view of the goings on. Sometimes the more rebellious kids will also sit in the back, thinking that they can get away with things, being as far away from the driver as possible, this way, we had the driver up front and me watching the kids from the back of the bus.

"There was one particular student who seemed to be a magnet for trouble, her name was Melenia, and she had always required extra attention. She would be sent to the counselor for cursing and swearing, and wore clothes that as school attire were questionable. On more than one occasion, she was sent home with a note about 'proper school dress' and 'proper deportment.'"

"Every two or three hundred miles the bus would stop at interstate rest areas for the bus occupants to stretch out their legs and attend to personal matters. We had been traveling for about six hours and the kids were restless, fifty more miles and we would be at a rest stop in South Georgia.

"A female student who I knew to be trustworthy came down the aisle to speak with me, she had a look of concern on her face." "Melenia has cigarettes, and she's hiding them under her shirt."

"Are you sure?" I asked. "Yes," she responded, "she's showing them to everyone."

The four people listening to Teach's story began shaking their heads.

"The bus stopped at the 'service area,' and pulled into a parking spot. I signaled for Melenia to come over and talk to me before the bus opened its doors. "Do you have something that maybe you shouldn't have?" I asked. "I Don't Know What You're Talking About," she said in a loud voice. "'I'll discuss it with you outside the bus,' I replied."

"She appeared distressed, and as the bus opened its doors, she pushed the other students aside and ran toward woods that lay behind the service building. I ran after her.

"I had run about fifty yards into these woods when I began catching up, I could see those cigarettes held tightly in her right hand."

"'Give Me That!'" I said with a raised voice, "I grabbed her arm to get the cigarette pack and we started to struggle. Both of us fell to the ground, into the dirt and mud, the cigarette pack flew out of her hand."

"And then she screamed a word that would change my life forever. Just one word, but a word I would later learn has the impact of lightning, the terror of thunder, and the force of a nuclear explosion."

"That word?" "RAPE!"

As soon as she screamed it, I heard a hustle coming from the woods where we had traveled from. Two large and well-fed men in military fatigues, one wearing a t-shirt that said 'Kiss A Redneck,' the other with a hat that said

'I'm Not Drunk, I Always Talk Like This,' came barreling through the brush."

"'GRAB HIM BUBBA,' screamed the one wearing the t-shirt, 'I'LL SIT ON HIS CHEST, BILLY BOB,' yelled the other, and I felt the crushing weight of three hundred and seventy-five pounds right on top of me."

"As I struggled to breathe, I could hear the one called 'Billy Bob' calming the tearful girl." "'Don't worry little lady, you're safe now, this slimeball is never gonna hurt you again and he's gonna pay for what he's done.'"

"With that the one called Bubba grabbed my right leg and thrust it over my back and at the same time, Billy Bob walked over and kicked me in the head."

"Holy Mother Mary, what a story," said Preach, as he shook his head.

"I'm not finished, but it's getting near suppertime and we best head out for the evening hash. I can finish the story later, besides it's the third Friday of the month."

The listeners reluctantly got to their feet, and Teach, Preach and Amos began their slow street train toward an evening meal.

"Can I tag along," asked Flathead, rubbing his scarred shoulder. "The more the merrier," responded Preach.

"What's so special about the 'third Friday?'" asked Flathead. "Come along young man and you'll learn a little bit about the poultry business." "You mean like what we're having for dinner?" The three others laughed, as Flathead looked puzzled.

CHAPTER SIX:
THE OLDEST SPECTATOR SPORT

They commenced walking west, back over the MacArthur Causeway toward Biscayne Boulevard and Downtown Miami. Preach began speaking with an admonition, "I'm not the greatest expert in the blood sport of cockfighting, but if I make a mistake, Teach here, and Amos here, can correct me," he looked at his companions as he spoke.

"From what I understand, cockfighting's been around forever." "That's right," responded Teach, "the Persians used to fight roosters six thousand years ago." "You should know," said Amos, "You was probably there." "Yes, and I still haven't collected my bet." They all laughed.

"Now in order to have a proper fight, you've got to have a proper rooster," said Preach.

"Them fightin roosters is called 'gamecocks,'"

"Why don't you just finish the story, Amos? you'd probably tell it better than me anyway."

"A fightin rooster is a special two-year old rooster, called a 'battle cock,' mean and ornery, it wants to be the only stud in the chicken house, it don't want nothing to do with any competition. It'll kill another rooster, peck out its eyes and shred him to pieces, he don't show him no mercy."

"What does this all have to do with the third Friday of the month?" asked the man dressed in military fatigues. "Don't worry, I'll be gettin to that," responded Amos.

"It takes a special fightin rooster, and different breeds have different natures, some say that the best fighting rooster is the Flarry Eyed Grey, others say the Green Legged Hatch."

Teach began to speak, "There are over two hundred types of roosters in America, of these, five different types are pretty much what they use in all the cockfights. There's the Lemon Hatch, smart rooster and tough fighter, the Husley rooster, seen in a lot of cock fights, the sweater rooster, sleek with long black tail feathers, the Mclean cocks, called 'power cocks,' fine physical specimens but not too bright."

"There's the roundheads, including the famous Judge Lacy Jasper Roundheads, and then there's my favorite, the Flarry Eyed Grey, not the biggest or the strongest, just the smartest and handsomest rooster that God ever put on the Earth."

"Okay, I get it, but what has this all got to do with anything?"

Preach explained, "Every third Friday of the month, we have a grand event under the bridge, upwards of one hundred and fifty people crowd in to watch the best cockfights on planet Earth."

"You've got to be kidding me,"

"Young man, I'm telling you that it's a sight for sore eyes, the bettors and participants come loaded and ready for the show."

"Where do they park? How come they aren't discovered?" asked Flathead.

"That's the beauty of it," Teach explained, Friday nights are always busy and crowded in Miami, people go to SeaSide, the tourist mall over here," he pointed to his left. "Thousands travel over the causeway to Miami Beach, there's excitement everywhere. The cops are too busy with all of that to notice that anything's going on, most of the rooster breeders bring their best birds."

"They take fishing rods and large tackle boxes as if they're going fishing off the causeway bridge, these tackle boxes are really chicken crates. They park downtown and walk across the bridge with their champions, some show up on boats and unload right under the bridge, it's quite a sight," Teach continued.

"We've dug out a cockpit where the rooster's fight, it's covered up most of the time, but we get it ready for the big event."

"Can you make any money?" asked Flathead. "Make any money?" Amos replied, "No Brains won so much money at one match that he started looking to buy a car, but they wouldn't give him no license, since he had about a thousand drunk driving arrests."

They soon found themselves at Saint Maria's Home For The Destitute, where they sat down for dinner.

"At least they don't mix the food here," observed Teach. "Yeah," responded Amos, "It's hard to mix a hamburger with anything else but ketchup."

"Who do you think has the upper hand tonight?" asked Preach.

"Well, I'm putting my money on that new rooster, Number Thirty-Four," Amos replied, "they don't be givin fightin cocks names, but I be hearin this one be nicknamed called 'Rojo Alabama,' you know, 'Alabama Red.'"

"I've heard something about that rooster," responded Teach, "Isn't that one of Judge Lacy's inventions?" "Judge who?" asked Flathead.

"Back in some place called Jasper Alabama, this old time Judge raised the best fighting cocks in the world. Lacy Roundhead Roosters were fearsome and vicious, but probably the greatest fighting rooster of all time was the legendary Two Toed Cock.

Judge Lacy had bought this small four-pound yellow cock from some guy in Birmingham. They say he paid 'five dollars,' it was a red eyed, pea combed, yellow legged rascal. Unimpressive looking, he was meaner than a junkyard dog on steroids, and he showed his opponents no mercy, ripping them apart seven times in a row."

"Judge Lacy bred this rascal with his other fighting roosters, creating the breed known as Lacy Roundheads, this Alabama bird is a direct relative of that Two Toed Bastard."

"Saints preserve us, mercy may not be in the picture tonight," said Preach

"No," stated Amos, "but a big payoff may take its place instead." "I don't have much money to put down on a cockfight," said Flathead.

"I can spot you twenty dollars," answered Teach, "but if you win big, you're gonna have to pay me back." "I fully intend to pay you back, with interest." Everyone smiled.

Their meal finished they commenced their walk back to the bridge.

Chapter Seven:
Dinner

"So, what's the end of the story," asked Flathead as he looked at Teach, "What happened to put you living under a bridge?"

"You mean after they put me in that hellhole of a jail in South Georgia?"

"Yeah, after that."

"Well, my situation made the papers all over Georgia and Miami,

"They quoted the two Bozo's who found me with the girl," "'Yeah,' said Billy Bob Hiram, "'I caught him right in the act, Bubba here subdued him and gave him a little taste of Southern Justice.'"

"No matter how hard I protested, they all just laughed, you'd think that the fact that I had been 'Teacher of the Year' would have given me some credibility, but the newspapers used that fact against me. They all blared banner headlines like; 'Teacher Of The Year Charged With Assaulting Student' 'Another Embarrassment As Teacher Violates The Public Trust.' 'Richard Bradford Should Fry.'"

"They were talking about me all over the news, with newscasters shaking their heads, editorials from people who wanted to lynch me. One guy wanted to 'cut off' my private parts right then and there, so they put me into solitary confinement, 'for your own protection.'"

"They began talking to my students, both present and former. They asked them all kinds of questions, questions like, 'Was he different from the other teachers?'" "They would respond with things like, 'He really paid a lot of attention to us, more than the other teachers.' They used that against me too, they called me a 'pervert.'"

"They decided to file charges in Federal Court and they sent me to Miami where the trip began." "Federal charges, holy shit," said Amos. "Yeah, they really wanted to fry me. Because we had crossed state lines, they charged me with something called the 'Mann Act.'"

"What in Lord's mercy is that?" asked Preach. "Well, it's a law against something called '"white slavery."' Amos started chuckling, "There don't seem to be no laws against black slavery." "It isn't funny, it's a law against the 'interstate transportation of females for immoral purposes.'"

"They acted as if I had planned this whole trip out myself in order have sex with this student."

"Then they threw in this other charge, something called 'Sex Trafficking Of Children By Force, Fraud Or Coercion.'" "Since she was only fourteen years old, that charge called for imprisonment of ten years to life."

"Did you have an attorney?" asked Preach.

"They still hadn't assigned me a lawyer and it was over a month since I'd been arrested. I'd sit in the jail and watch television shows that would come on the air and say things like 'In the criminal justice system, sexually based offenses are considered especially horrible. In the big city the trained detectives who investigate these depraved felonies are members of a takedown unit devoted to stopping these maniacs, and here are their stories.'"

"I watched this and almost broke down crying, 'Who'll represent the innocent people, like those wrongfully charged . . . ? Who'll represent me . . . ? Who'll Represent Me . . . ?'"

"Soon I found out, I was sent an overworked and underpaid lawyer in the employ of the Federal Public Defender. He gave me the news, seems that they had done a 'physical examination of the victim' and she showed 'clear signs of previous sexual activity.'"

"What does the girl say? Does she say that I 'raped her???'" "From what I understand, she's saying that you and she had a thing going, that you used to meet with her privately and that's when it would happen," he replied.

"This is pure bullshit, sure I met with her, but it was to discuss her foul language and her improper and revealing clothing. The lawyer looked at me as if I had made a confession."

"The lawyer told me that they took a DNA sample of the girl and supposedly one from me as well, when I was in that small jail up in Georgia, he asked if I 'remembered?'"

"All I remember was being in this hot and unairconditioned rat hole when some supposed medical technologist swabbed my mouth with a Q-tip."

"That's how they get the samples," he told me.

"How long before the DNA results come back?"

"It will be around six weeks," replied the lawyer.

"You mean I'm stuck in here another six weeks? What about bond?" "As a dangerous sexual offender who planned the rape of a fourteen-year-old girl, it's not likely that you will ever be released on bond, you're just going to have to wait."

"Well at least they're going to get those results and find out that I'm innocent." "Boy was I a dope."

"What about your wife and kids?" asked Flathead, "didn't they come out to visit you?"

"They did, but it wasn't the same, my wife acted strange, it was as if she didn't trust me, as if she thought I was lying. After the DNA results came out, she stopped communicating with me all together."

"My lawyer had come back with the news and the results showed a positive match. He explained that they excluded everyone else, he said that there was a 'one in a billion' or so chance that someone else was responsible for having had a sexual relationship with that girl'"

"According to my lawyer, this was a very strong case, they had eye witnesses, not only the two men who 'caught me in the act,' but all of the students and others who watched me chase the girl into the woods. Further, he alluded to my own statement that I had 'met with the girl privately.'"

"Look," he said, "You're going to have to face the facts." "But I'm innocent!" I protested, "I chased that girl to get that pack of cigarettes away from her."

"He looked at me skeptically, then he gave me the 'good news,'"

"The government was prepared to make me a plea offer, they were willing to drop the 'white slavery charge,' if I plead to the 'sex by coercion/fraud charge.' "He told me that I 'had no other choice.' "They've got a high conviction rate, particularly in cases involving DNA, close to one hundred percent," he said, "absent this plea, the Government was prepared to go to trial and upon conviction ask for life in prison."

"'How can these low life liars, scumbags and slimeballs do this to me!' I screamed, "I'M INNOCENT!!!'"

"Holy Mother of Mary," said Preach, "So what did you do next?"

Well, my lawyer had one trick up his sleeve, he was going to try to have the DNA results excluded because the people employed at the facility had no real training in science or anything like that. He was also going to ask the judge to appoint an expert and have the government provide money to re-test the DNA at another facility.

"So did the judge grant your request," asked Flathead.

"I remember the Judge's words well," responded Teach, "'The facility that the government already used is a well-respected scientific laboratory, one that this selfsame court has determined on countless occasion to be reliable and trustworthy. As far as a re-test by your own expert is concerned, I am afraid that the expense of such a request in this atmosphere of budgetary restraint will create an undue burden on the system. Motion Denied, prepare to be in trial this coming Monday.'"

"What about the undue burden on you?"

"That ain't the half of it, I spent several sleepless nights mulling the whole thing over, then I thought about my children. I knew I was innocent but the prospect of never seeing them again hit me hard. Not a praying man, I began to read the Bible, and like the story of Job, I decided that if this is where God wanted to put me, well here I am. When Monday came around, I told my lawyer that I had 'changed my mind' and would in fact take the Government's offer."

"If that ain't shit," responded Amos.

"Came time for sentencing, the Assistant United States Attorney called me the 'worst piece of human slime' that ever walked the face of the earth.'"

"My court appointed attorney fought hard for me. That nice judge, the one who denied motion for retesting because it was 'too expensive,' gave me the minimum, ten years in Federal Prison."

"I wonder how much that cost the government?" asked Preach.

"While in Prison, my wife divorced me. Now that I'm a convicted sex offender, I'm prohibited from having any contact with children, including my own."

"When they released me, I had no place to go and no money to go there with. The sex offender laws forced me to live at least a half mile away from the schools, bus stops and city parks. They sent me to the Julia Tuttle Sex Offender Colony a little past Thirty-Six Street."

"What's that?" asked Flathead.

"That's a group of people," answered Preach, "that live under the Julia Tuttle Causeway. It's been compared to a "Leper Colony."

"Julia Tuttle was one of the founders of Miami," responded Teach, "In her honor, they named this bridge after her and to further honor her, they put a sex offender colony under that very bridge.

"I wasn't going to stay there with those people, so Preach convinced me to come live under, the MacArthur Causeway."

"It's got better views," responded Preach. Preach and Teach both laughed.

Chapter Eight:
The Grand Event

It was a little after 7 p.m. when the four of them came back within sight of the MacArthur, they could see that something was happening. As they got near the area under the bridge where they lived, they encountered people milling around and talking excitedly.

Once in a while a speedboat or pleasure craft would put up to the spit under the bridge, and three or four occupants with crates and boxes would disembark onto the sand. Others would arrive after walking from across the top of the bridge, some holding fishing poles, some holding large boxes with holes visible on the top and sides.

Teach walked up to one man dressed in a white linen jacket, wearing a Panama hat and smoking a fat cigar.

"Ola Amigo!" said Teach, "How's the Alabama Killer doing?" "He's looking real horny tonight," answered the man in the jacket, "I think he's gonna please the ladies."

"I feel sorry for any rooster that gets in his way," replied Teach.

"Who's that?" asked Flathead. "That's 'El Cabron' 'The Bastard,'" replied Amos. "He's the meanest son of a bitch that ever set hands on a gamecock. He's the owner of several champion birds, including that new one, Number

Thirty-Four, I'm told it's a killer bird."

"Why do they call him 'The Bastard,'" asked Flathead. "Well for one thing," replied Amos, "he makes his birds fight until they win or until they die. Some owners will call the match if their bird is too injured to continue, but El Cabron will make his birds fight until the pit is bloody with the remains of either his opponent's or his own bird."

"But I'll tell something," said Preach, "It's usually the poor bird that faces his gamecock that loses."

As the four of them walked toward the center area of the spit, they encountered men setting up lights. A scale with tripod legs sat ten yards from a pit where the gamecocks were to fight. "What's the scale for?" asked Flathead. "That's so they can weigh the roosters, roosters are placed in matches according to their weight."

"What time do the matches begin?" Teach asked a man setting up the lights. He turned and responded, "The first match is set for 9 p.m., there are going to be ten matches in total. The last match will be the championship match against Number Twenty-Six, that bird people call 'Crazy Shit,' the green legged hatch owned by Dr. Severin."

Teach turned to the others with him, "You know they say that the doctor feeds his birds Xanax, Steroids and who knows what, the same shit that made that monkey go crazy that was in the news for ripping a woman's face off."

"Which bird is slated to fight in the championship round with Crazy Shit?" Teach asked the man. "El Cabron has paid the one-thousand- dollar entry fee, Number Thirty-Four going to be the challenger."

By now, the spit of sand under the bridge was crowded with upwards of two hundred people. Lights had been set up around a lighted pit that had been dug out of the sand, and whose sides were reinforced with wood planking.

A man wearing a hat with a feather was taking note of bets. People would raise their hands, denoting with their fingers the amount they were risking and yelling out the number of the bird they favored.

"The winners all share in a percentage of the money put up by the losers,"

Teach explained, "that's after the house takes its ten percent off of the top. You can make side bets too, like how long the match is going to last, there's a lot of money to be made."

"Or you can lose your shirt," replied Preach.

"The big money goes to the owner of the winning rooster, they split the money the house gets."

"Last call for bets," said the man in the hat. "Hey Teach, aren't you going to bet on the match?" asked Amos "No." he responded, "I'm saving my money for the championship round." "I guess I'll do the same." "What about Preach?" asked Flathead, "Aren't you betting?"

"He doesn't bet," responded Amos, "He just prays for the souls of the damned who lay their money down to watch two poor animals tear each other to pieces."

A crowd of bettors surrounded the pit as the first two contestants were being prepped by their owners. Each had razor sharp spurs of two- inch length, attached to their legs by red leather bands, and both fighting cocks had been dubbed, their red wattle, and red comb trimmed off so that neither would be at a disadvantage.

"What are those dangerous looking things on their legs?" asked Flathead. "Those are sharpened spurs called knives," responded Teach, "The fights here follow the Cuban rules, the knives are natural rooster spurs, sharpened like razors, then attached to the gamecock's legs with leather fasteners.

"One more minute to go!" said the man in the hat, and with those words the first two roosters were put within sight of each other near opposite ends of the pit. One was a small colorful rooster, the other was mostly brown. "That's a bantam gamecock," Teach, pointed to the colorful one, "The other is some kind of mix."

Both gamecocks were set in the pit beak to beak. A man produced a bell and clacked it with a gong.

Immediately the brown rooster gained the advantage, attacking, kicking, flailing its wings, and pecking at the head of the colorful bantam. Wings spread and legs furiously working, he continued to peck at the colorful rooster's head. "There goes one eye," Amos spoke to Teach as blood spewed from the side of the bantam's head, covering his feathers with red blood, cackles and screeches emanated from the pit.

"There goes the other," Teach observed, as the poor and now defenseless rooster endured an onslaught by the brown monster. "That brown bird be like the Brown Bomber," said Amos, "he be showin no mercy."

After another couple minutes of brutal slaughter, the bantam lay down and made a mild clucking noise with its mouth. Another twenty seconds and the bird ceased all activity.

"The Winner!" screamed announcer, "Lucky Number Thirteen!" The owner of the Bantam walked into the pit and kicked his dead bird with the words, "God damn bird, you're going to make for some good dog food!" Several in attendance laughed, as if what he said was funny. Preach, Teach and Amos just kept quiet.

"If this is what humanity is about, I've got a lot more praying to do," observed Preach.

The next matches went pretty much along the same lines, it was as if the birds were fed into meat grinders. One bird would gain the advantage and maul the other bird senseless, it would peck out its eyes and slice through its body with the sharp spurs, inevitably, a bloody carcass would writhe in pain as it exhausted its last life's breath.

All the while, bettors would cheer and scream as the roosters fought to the bitter end, "Maul Him!" "Peck Out His Eyes!" "Slice Off His Head!" Screams and even laughter came from all directions.

"Finally," screamed the announcer, "it's time for the main event. The challenger, Number Thirty-Four, Rojo Alabama, the Jasper Roundhead, will be fighting the undefeated champion, Number Twenty-Six, Crazy Shit, the green legged hatch."

"Here's where we put our money down," Teach looked at Flathead and Amos, "I'm going for the Jasper Roundhead. "You must be whacked out," responded Amos, "that bird hasn't got a chance against Twenty-Six, not with all the drugs and steroids that bird's pumped up with, "I'm putting my money on Crazy Shit. "How bout you, Flathead?" asked Teach. "I'll put my money on the Roundhead." "You'll lose it all," said Amos. "Hell, it ain't mine anyway," answered Flathead, "So what's to lose?"

As the man with the hat walked by, Teach raised two fingers, "Two Hundred Dollars on Number Thirty-Four." Flathead next blurted, "I'll take twenty on the same bird." Amos, though slightly resignedly, said to the man, "I'll bet a hundred on the roundhead as well." Then he looked at Teach, "If I done lose my money, you ain't getting no inheritance." "I always thought that you'd outlive me anyway," chuckled Teach.

"One more minute to go," screamed the man taking bets, "This is the big one, so put your money down."

Around the pit with their gamecocks ready were El Cabron and Dr. Severin. Dr. Severin appeared calm and proud, like a man expecting something as inevitable as tomorrow's sunrise.

El Cabron, on the other hand, spoke encouragement to his black and brown bodied bird, with white feather's emanating from the tail, "You can do it, you're the man."

"Ten nine eight seven six five four three two one," "The Fight Is On!" screamed the announcer. The two birds who had been lifted into the pit, face to face, went right after each other with a viciousness that overshadowed all of the other matches. These birds showed a malevolence that was beyond description, the only question being whether brute force as a survival mechanism can outweigh such concepts as mercy and flight from danger.

The green legged hatch wildly directed its beak at the Alabama rooster's body and head, both birds jumping wildly at each other, both squawking in either zeal or agony, it was impossible to tell.

This happened again and again as the green legged bird continually thrust its beak toward Number Thirty-Four's eyes, but this is when things began to get interesting. As the green hatch went at Thirty-Four for the fifth time, the Alabama bird did something totally unexpected. With a quick upward thrust of its legs, It sliced Twenty-Six's neck, sliced it so badly that blood started spurting out."

"He Roped A Dope," screamed Amos, "He Roped A Dope!" The crowd went wild. "I don't think this is going to last long," said Teach, "I think he got the carotid artery." As the blood continued to spurt from the green legged hatch's neck, its movements got slower. Seeing a chance, Rojo Alabama quickly finished the job, slicing at the dying bird, pecking out its bird's eyes. It fell to ground mortally injured, breathing it's last."

A cheer emanated from a small portion of the crowd, while the vast majority gasped in shock and disappointment. "That's the betting game," said Teach to Flathead, "Sometimes you win and sometimes you lose, but it's a lot more fun to win!" "Sure is," responded Amos, "Sure is."

Chapter Nine:

A Small Side Trip

The next morning as the four headed out for breakfast, Amos counted his money "Ten to one, Ten to one! Thank you Jesus, Jesus thank you!" he said as he kissed the wad.

"I don't think its Jesus you should thank," said Preach.

"This time we're having a high-quality meal," responded Teach, "All on me." "We're heading to Mack's Stone Crabs on the Beach!" "They're not gonna let us in, at least not dressed like we is," said Amos, "Sides, don't we need no reservation?"

"First let's head over to Burdocks Department Store in Downtown, we'll get some duds, and then head out."

As they rolled through the door of Burdocks, a security guard approached. "Can I help you gentlemen?" asked the man. "No, we're beyond help," said Amos, "Just show us where the fine men's clothing is?" He then slipped the security guard a twenty.

"Over here gentlemen," replied the guard, "just let me know if you need help with anything."

Amos quickly picked out a green suit, patent leather shoes, a white shirt, and a hat with a green feather protruding from the band. Teach dressed more conservatively with a sport coat, new pants and a shirt with an open collar. Flathead bought a shirt and pants.

"Say," said Preach to a saleslady, "You haven't got any clerical garb perhaps?" "In fact, we do," answered the sales lady, "Come right this way." Preach soon found what he was looking for, a new shirt, clerical collar, pants and shoes.

"Now I look like a proper man of the cloth," he said as he exited the dressing room.

"That will be one thousand, three hundred and sixty-seven dollars and fifty-two cents," said the cashier. "No problem," answered Amos, "this man's good for it," and he pointed at Teach. Teach took the money out of his pocket and paid the bill.

As they started to exit the store, they passed the perfume and cologne department. "Free sample? Free sample?" said a lady holding a tray with colorful cologne and perfume.

"Look," said Teach to the others, "If we're going to Mack's Stonecrabs, we can't smell like we're living under a bridge."

"I'll have some of that bottle with the stud horse on it," said Amos. "Sir," responded the lady, "you're funny." "That's a polo pony, not a stud horse." She sprayed a whiff toward his face, "Is that enough?" she asked. "No, give me another squirt," he answered. "Is that enough?" again the lady asked.

"Why don't you just give me that there bottle," and with that, he grabbed the cologne and commenced spraying it on his face, legs, arms and underarms.

"I'll just have a whiff," said Teach. "Us too ma'am," said Preach, standing next to Flathead. They departed Burdocks for the long walk back across the MacArthur Causeway to South Beach and Mack's Stonecrabs.

As they went along, Amos' head began to droop, it had been quite an evening and it was a long trip to the Beach, on the other side of the Causeway. Soon his eyes closed and he found himself in dreamland.

In a hazy transformation, he was transported back to the time that his trusty legs were his main mode of transportation, that time way back in his past when he was the life of the party. There were girlfriends aplenty and friends hanging around all the time. He was back to the time when he would party till the late hours, drinking, playing cards, fooling with the women.

Then there was the night his life changed forever, just as though it was yesterday, he was back at his nephew's house. There was a real party going on, plenty of drinks and plenty of females. The card games were fast and hot, just like the women.

The clock read two and his nephew called him over, "Hey Uncle Amos, here's some money for you to go make another liquor run." "Sure thing." As he walked out to his car, he saw that he had left the now dim headlights on. When he turned the key, the starter made a clicking noise.

"Damn," he muttered under his breath.

"Use my car, here the keys," said the nephew, as he tossed them to Amos.

As Amos started north up Biscayne Boulevard toward the liquor store, his phone rang. "Hey you listen here Citronella, we gonna connect up soon as I get back, you just remember that I'm the man, I'm the man." "Wait a minute, there's someone following me."

It was then that he saw the blue light.

"Damn."

"ROLL DOWN THE WINDOW MISTER!" Yelled the cop as he pointed the gun directly at Amos' head. As the dream commenced to a climax, he threw down his phone, opened the car door and began to run.

Loud shots rang out, as Amos woke up in a cold sweat.

"Dreaming back to the good old days?" asked Preach. "The days I was dreaming about weren't so good," he replied.

"If you want to tell us about it," went Preach, "It might make you feel better."

"Feel better, Bullshit! I'm just angry, just angry," tears started dripping down his face. "I done nothing to these people, yet they took away my right to walk, it was my right, wasn't it . . . my right to walk?

"My court appointed lawyer reads me the police report about when I was shot. Cops say, I was 'weaving in and out of the lanes' but all I remember was being on the telephone. The police report say that when they finally stopped me I refused to roll down the window, they say that I was talking and appeared annoyed."

"'Roll down the window, Mister!' was the words that the cops supposedly said," Amos chuckled, "Then they say that I rolled down the window partway, pointed at my phone and yelled at them 'Can't You See I'm On The Damn Telephone!'"

"Next thing I know they jerk open the car door."

"Courtesy is dead today," said Preach. "Sure is," replied Teach.

"When I look in their eyes, one thing runs through my mind. Run. Run fast as you can or you're a dead man. Cops said that I 'attacked them,' but that's bullshit. If I attacked them, how is it that I got shot in the back?"

"I had run about fifteen yards when they opened up with their guns. That's the last time I ever walked again." "Those bastards don't give a damn about anybody," said Teach.

"Well, it got even better, when they searched the car and found my nephew's stash in the tire compartment. They said that it was 'crack cocaine.'" "I didn't know nothing about no cocaine in no car, but they didn't give a shit, they said that I was 'a drug dealer running from the cops.'"

"When I was in the hospital, they give me the news that I would never walk again, then they come and arrest me, like I was gonna run off somewhere!" With those words, they approached the neon sign that read "Mack's Stonecrabs, America's Best."

Chapter Ten:
No Reservations Required

When the maitre d' saw the wheelchair led train approach, he called out to a nearby waitress, "You'd better stick here with me, this might get interesting."

As the four came closer, the maître d' and waitress were immediately struck with the pungent smell of high-end cologne mixed with the smell of dirty 'under the overpass' bridge living and sweat generated by two miles walk over a long causeway on a hot and steamy South Florida day.

"Can I help you gentlemen?" asked the maître d', "Do you have reservations?" "I do," answered Amos, "but I'm still gonna eat here anyway!" he replied, as the other three chuckled.

The maître d's expression remained the same.

"Can I have the name?" asked the man. "Amos," "Amos Haveaseat." "That's very funny Mr. Haveaseat, but I don't see your name on the reservation list."

"Maybe this will refresh your recollection," answered Amos, as he pulled a hundred dollar bill out of his pocket and gave it to the man.

"Right this way," gentlemen, "Bernina, give these men window seats." He then leaned and whispered into Bernina's ear, "and make sure the windows open wide so a nice breeze can freshen the air."

They sat down and the waitress came over, "What will it be, Gentlemen," How about some wine to start things out?"

"That sounds pretty good," said Teach, "what do you recommend?" "We have a fine California Sauvignon Blanc, but many prefer the CapoDimonte Pino Gris."

"We'll go with both," replied Amos, "that way we'll hedge our bets!"

"We'd best say a prayer before we eat," said Preach, "to thank the Lord for our new found bounty."

"Why don't you lead us?" asked Teach.

"Dear God, thank you for bringing us here today for this fine meal, a falsely disgraced schoolteacher, a paralyzed man in a wheelchair, a one-legged priest, and, he looked at Flathead, and a friend from the Carolinas, all humble servants who depend upon your grace and goodwill." They all said "Amen."

After consuming three full platters of stone crabs and the four bottles of wine, they sat back and relaxed. A loud grunt like "burp" emanated from Amo's mouth.

"You know they charged me with being a trafficker, they say there was more than fifty grams of crack cocaine in the baggie they found under the spare tire, that I was facing a minimum sentence of ten years in federal prison."

"You mean those same bastards who shot you in the back filed federal charges against you too?" asked Flathead.

"Damn right," responded Amos, "they knew they had done wrong, so they made sure that I paid double for something I never did. Not only would I never walk again, they put me in federal lockup for the next ten years of my life."

"They sent me a lawyer, and he explained to me that because there was crack cocaine along with the powder, that the sentencing level was something like a hundred to one. That it was some kind of racist thing to put black people in jail, cause it be mostly blacks who bake the crack rocks. White men snort the powder, so the law don't care too much about them."

"I told him that it wasn't my stash." "Whose stash is it?" the lawyer asked. "I don't know," I said, "but it sure as hell ain't mine."

"He didn't believe me."

"My lawyer told me about something called Sentencing Guidelines, that these people in the federal system use some kind of numbers that they add up to determine how many years in jail you stay."

"I ain't no number," I told my lawyer, "I'm a human being, and I'm being punished for something I never even done." All three of the others shook their heads.

"Don't worry," said the lawyer, "You'll probably get the ten-year minimum, I'll argue that you've been punished enough, not being able to walk and all."

"Like he was doing me a favor, asking for ten years, there just ain't no justice in this world."

"In this world you will have tribulation, trials and sorrow," replied Preach. All of the others shook their heads in agreement.

"So, they gave me ten years in jail, they robbed me of my ability to walk and gave me ten years in jail. I admit I'd been drinking, and maybe they should have charged me with that, but ten years in jail and no more legs, what did I do to deserve that?"

As they got ready to depart, they called the waitress over with the bill. 'Five hundred and sixty-three dollars and fifty-nine cents,' not including gratuity. "I'll take care of this one," said Amos.

"No," said Teach, "this one's mine as well."

They departed the restaurant, and commenced walking back to their home under the MacArthur Causeway.

Chapter Eleven:

AN APPARITION

As they started leaving the parking lot, a barely audible 'clucking' noise permeated the air. "Did you hear that?" asked Amos. All four stopped in their tracks, as it started getting louder, "If I didn't know better, I'd say that that was a rooster," said Teach.

"Do you two hear anything?" he asked Flathead and Preach.

Then, just like an apparition, it appeared.

"There he is!" screamed Amos, "sitting right on top of that Ferrari, and it's a Flarry Eyed Grey!" "That makes sense," replied Teach, "The symbol of Ferrari is a horse, and a horse is a farm animal. This rooster feels right at home on that car."

"Probably likes the red color as well," observed Preach.

All four slowly surrounded the car. "Here chicky chicky," 'Here chicky chicky," all spoke at once. As they got closer, Amos produced an old smelly t-shirt from a bag that was hanging on the back of his wheelchair. "If we catch him, I'll put him in this here shirt."

When they came within a half a foot, the rooster bolted for parts unknown. "Well, we gave it our best shot," said Teach, "It just wasn't meant to be."

"Did you see where he went?" asked Amos. "No, but it was probably when he saw the t-shirt that he ran, the smell enough would have probably killed him," responded Teach.

"We best start back," said Preach, "it's been a long day and we're all a little tired."

They had walked almost a half mile toward home, and were in sight of the Capone mansion when Flathead looked back, "Hey guys," he said, "Isn't that your rooster that's following us?" "Holy mother of Mary, it sure looks like it is," answered Preach, "You guys stay here, if you want a rooster to be your friend, I'll show you how it's done."

Preach walked over to the bird. "How are you doing little fellow?" The rooster cackled a sort of response. "Would you like to be my friend? I'd sure like to be your friend." The rooster cackled again and came closer.

Preach began petting the bird's head and scratching his neck.

"Holy St. Francis of Assisi, I don't believe what I'm seeing," said Teach.

"You know," said Preach, still addressing the bird, "it's a long walk back across this long stretch of land, why don't I just give you a lift? Just hop right up here on my shoulder."

Without hesitation the bird hopped up on Preach's right shoulder. Preach turned around and began walking back to the others.

"If this ain't a sight for sore eyes, I don't know what is," said Amos. A paraplegic black man in a wheelchair being pushed by a schoolteacher, accompanied by a man with a military crewcut and a one- legged priest with a rooster on his shoulder."

As they walked toward the causeway, cars slowed down and drivers gawked. After walking a half hour, they made it back to their home on the sand spit under the bridge.

Several residents of the bridge community began to point and stare. One Lip and Ebenezer walked over and assessed the situation.

"Looks like this rooster is gonna need a home," observed Amos. "I know where there's an abandoned chicken crate," replied Ebenezer, "you just wait right here."

Meanwhile, One Lip produced a canvas feed bag and slowly walked up behind Preach, the rooster still on his shoulder. In the flash of an eye, the Flarry Eyed Grey was in the bag, a loud "squawk!" emanated from the captured bird.

"Here, put him in this abandoned crate," said Ebenezer. "Boy you guys are sure lucky, that's the best-looking gamecock I've ever seen."

"He's still a little scrawny and needs some beefing up," replied Teach. "What are you going to call the bird?" sputtered One Lip.

"We caught him near Al Capone's mansion," said Amos, "So that's what we'll call him, 'Al Capone.'"

"That's a good name," answered Teach. "That's a good name."

"It's been a long day," said Preach, "let's get a good night's sleep."

Chapter Twelve:
Enhancing Human Existence

It was 4:00 a.m. when the first sign of trouble raised its nasty head. "COCK A DOODLE DOO," "COCK A DOODLE DOO!!!!"

"Holy shit," can you shut that damn bird up came grumblings from residents under the bridge."

"COCK A DOODLE DOO, COCK A DOODLE DOO!!!!"

"I know what'll stop him," replied another man, "some good whole grain stuffing, lemon herb marinade, and Martha White Biscuits."

"Don't you be rassing my bird," Amos shot back, "he be a fightin bird, not an eating bird."

"Well why don't you shut the damn thing up?"

Preach walked over to the homemade cage, "Hello little fellow, how you doing today?" The rooster seemed to immediately calm down.

"I'm going to let us all get a little more sleep," said Preach to the rooster, "a well-rested rooster is a happy rooster." He took his blanket and covered the cage.

"He'll think it's night," replied Teach, "that'll stop him." The rooster crowed again, but with the blanket covering the cage, the volume was far less."

The wheelchair led train headed off for an early breakfast. "Looks like it's the Christian House of Charity for this morning's meal," said Teach, "we're running through money faster than Colonel Sander's runs through chickens, and if we can't keep him quiet in the morning, he may be on the Colonel's menu."

"Now don't say that," replied Amos, "we got one chicken, err rooster, whose depending upon us for support, we gotta find us some high-quality chicken feed and proper livin facilities. We've got to get Al in tip top shape, ifn he's ever gonna be a fighter, I knows that this bird's gonna do great things and we've got to make sure he knows he's appreciated."

"There's a feed store I know of way down south in the Redlands," said Teach, "we may have to take the Metrorail and then transfer to a bus to get us there." "I'm game for the trip," replied Flathead, "besides, I'd like to see a little bit of the city. I hopped a train to get here, and haven't really seen much of Miami."

"Miami is a lost place with lots of lost people," said Preach, "but to some it's a tropical paradise." The group of four men made their way down Northeast Second Avenue, soon they found themselves at the Christian House of Charity. The line of poor and displaced people waiting for a meal stretched on for two blocks.

Inevitably, they made it through the door and to the serving line. "So how you guy's doing today?" asked the lady behind the serving counter, "looks like you've got someone new with you."

"This here is Flathead," replied Amos, "he heard about your fine food all the way from the Carolinas, and hopped a train to get here."

"Welcome to Florida," said the serving lady, "My name is Esmerelda."

"Glad to meet you," replied Flathead, "what's the special today?"

"He had to ask" said Teach, "sometimes it's better when they just surprise us."

Esmerelda looked at Teach and snickered, "you got two choices," she responded, "Bean curd and scrambled egg, or scrambled egg and bean curd."

"I'll have the scrambled egg and bean curd," said Flathead, "I've learned never to ask for the first thing on the menu."

The Cockfight

"Good thinking," said Preach, "I find that they always save their best cooking as a surprise."

As they sat down, Apache came by. "Congratulations on your new fighting cock, that was one heck of a lucky find."

"Oh, he's just friend who came by to say hello," said Teach, "we just want to treat him like an honored guest." "Yep," we gonna find him some high-class chicken feed and all," said Amos.

"Who's that girl asking questions?" Teach asked Apache, alluding to a good-looking woman with brunette hair and blue eyes, carrying a note clip and talking to various people as they ate their morning meal.

"Oh, that's the lady from the Florida Department of Social Services, she shows up here once in a while."

After approximately ten minutes, she made her way to where the group was eating.

"Hi, I'm with the Florida Department of Social Services, and I'm here to see how I can help you. Do you mind if I ask you a few questions?"

"You can help me if you knows a good horse be coming in at Tropical Downs," answered Amos.

"No, I don't think I do," she responded, "but I might be able to arrange some medical care. Also looks like that wheelchair of yours needs some new padding."

"Well, my hind quarters do hurt sometimes," replied Amos, "I'd like to get me one of them 'power chairs.'"

"Yeah, that way I wouldn't have to strain my back, pushing you all over town," responded Teach, "or strain my ears listening to your bullshit," they all chuckled.

"How about you, sir," how can I help you? "Just call me Rick," he responded, "and what can I call you?" "My name is Debra," she answered.

"Now what kind of help are you offering," he looked at her with questioning eyes? "Not that kind of help," she replied.

Next, she addressed Preach, "Why are you here, pastor?" "I'm here to save these men's souls from Hell and Damnation."

"So how you doing?" asked Amos.

"You're a work in progress, but with God all things are possible," responded Preach.

Addressing Flathead last, he told her little, "I'm just here visiting from North Carolina. Don't need any help, thanks anyway."

"It's time for us to start working our way south," said Preach, "thanks for your concern."

"No problem," she replied, "I just want to make a difference."

"Well, you sure have," replied Teach, "will I, uh, we, uh, see you again?" "I certainly hope so," she answered, "I certainly hope so."

As the group made its way toward the Government Center Metrorail Station, Flathead nudged Teach. "You seem like you've got a thing for that girl," he chuckled. "Naw," responded Teach, "Naw, I just want to help her 'make a difference.'"

They used the elevator to head upward to the train level of the Metrorail Station, fifty or sixty people spread out across the rail, waiting for the train to arrive. "Stand Back, Stand Back," said the recorded announcement, "A Southbound Train Is Now Approaching."

As the train skidded to a halt, the four travelers entered one of the final cars. They sat down near the back.

Preach began to dose off to sleep. It had been a long day and night, and he began to talk in his sleep. "No!" "Don't Go There!" "I'll Save You!!!"

"Hey, wake up Preach, you're talking in your sleep." "Just reliving the days gone by."

"You know," said Teach, "you hear everyone else's story, but no-one ever listens to you. Maybe you ought to tell us what's eatin you?"

"How is it that a one-legged Irish Priest finds himself living under a bridge in Downtown Miami?"

"It's a long story, and I'm not sure you'd want to hear it all." "Sure, we would," answered Teach, "besides, we've got some time to kill before we reach the feed store."

Chapter Thirteen:
The American Dream

"I was born in Dunmurry, located in County Antrim Northern Ireland. Me father was an engineer, used to tinker with automobiles," said Preach.

"In 1975, he was introduced to a man by the name of John Delorean, had some kind of an idea for a new kind of car, something that would really 'shake up' the automobile world."

"You mean that stainless steel sports car?" asked Teach, "the one that was put together in the United Kingdom."

"They called it a DMC-12," Preach replied, "and me father was one of the engineers that put it together."

"Mr. Delorean really liked the job me father did, he had high respect for his talent. My father had a high opinion of Mr. Delorean as well. 'He's a great example of American entrepreneurship,'" said me dad, "'I'll follow that man anywhere.'"

"And follow him he did, in 1980, he asked me father to come and take a permanent position with the design department in Detroit Michigan. Our whole family, me father, me mother, me sister Erin, and myself, left Ireland for a new life, a life for which we had great expectations.

"So, what happened," asked Flathead, "Did your family find the American

Dream?"

"Sit back young man," answered Preach, "there's a lot more to the story."

The train slid into Dadeland South, the farthest southbound stop. "We've got to transfer onto bus 35," Teach pointed out, "that will get us to our destination."

"What's that food I smell cooking?" asked Flathead. "That's Smokey's," the finest barbecue restaurant in America," replied Teach, "We can hit that for lunch on the way back."

After navigating through crowds of people, they found themselves on the lower bus level, waiting for Bus Number 35."

"How do all of these people get around this city?" asked Flathead, "there's no space, everyone is packed in like a big sardine can."

"This place be about as crazy as it gets," answered Amos, "ain't no peace and quiet for no one no how."

"There she is, Bus 35," said Preach. As they boarded the bus, Teach and Flathead lifted Amos and his wheelchair onboard.

They rolled Amos to the back of the bus and took seats around him. Once the bus commenced its bumpy ride, Flathead asked if Preach could continue the story.

"We've got a little time till we reach our exit near Southwest 184th Street," answered Preach, "so I'll tell you a little more."

Chapter Fourteen:

A Modern American Business Model

"Mr. Delorean was very good to me father, he said that he was a 'trusted employee.' 'Sean,' he would say, 'here's a briefcase locked full of important documents, I trust you to please deliver it to some gentlemen. We'll fly you out in my private plane.'"

"He would send me dad to all types of exotic places where he would meet all kinds of interesting people. Me dad would tell us that he was on some kind of trip to 'Medellin Columbia' and that he had to deliver a 'package' or something like that down there.'" "Mr. D had told him it was 'Something to do with financing.'"

"We supposed that perhaps they were looking to set up some kind of car dealership or something like that down there, but it wasn't the kind of dealership our family was thinking about.

"When he arrived, they took him by jeep, far into the jungle, there were soldiers all around, carrying automatic weapons. He was led into a Quonset hut where he met an important looking gentleman."

"'Hola Senior, I see you've arrived with the agreed upon advance.'"

"Me dad would just smile, and hand over the briefcase. Next, two men with machine guns would escort a third man who came out of a back room. He handed me father a larger, fatter briefcase, and told him to 'wish El Carro Hombre good luck.'"

"When me dad got back, he'd give the package to Mr. Delorean, he didn't know anything about what was in the suitcase he was returning with, except that sometimes a little white powder would spill out of it. Mr. Delorean was always excited upon me dad's return."

"Jumping Jehoshaphat," said Amos, "Didn't he have a clue about what was going on?"

"Not a clue," responded Preach, "at least not until the big event."

"I remember coming home from me high school when Mom, Dad and Sister were sitting round the table moping." "Who died," I asked? "No one died," said me mother, "only our 'American Dream.'"

"Look at the t.v."

"'John Delorean, Successful Automotive Entrepreneur And Car Design Genius Has Been Arrested For Drug Trafficking,'" spoke the newsman, "'The Federal Government Has Charged Him In A Twenty-four Million Dollar Deal Involving 55 Pounds Of Cocaine.'"

"We're coming to our stop," said Teach, as he reached up and pressed the long rubber stripping that activated a bell, letting the bus driver know that they needed to be let off.

"Do we have chicken feed? Only the best there is," replied the husky man behind the counter of the feed store, "Turbo Rooster High Octane Brand, is guaranteed to turn your rooster into a ripped bird, he'll have six pack abs and the best-looking hind quarters in the poultry world."

"High octane, high octane, I like that," said Amos.

"Does the rooster have a name?" asked the man. "Al Capone," responded Teach, "but we found him sitting on top of a Ferrari."

"Well, there you go," replied the man, "How can you go wrong?"

"We've got another question to ask," said Preach, "how can we stop this nice fine bird of ours from being an alarm clock?"

"Or a featured item on Colonel Sander's menu?" added Teach

"Oh the 4:30 a.m. special," replied the man. "4:00 a.m., in this case."

"Well, the best answer is this here special chicken coop, it's got an upper berth near the top of the cage. The bird can't cock a doodle if he can't stretch his neck out.

"This special cage is designed so that the bird can't stretch out his neck in the morning and crow, during the day, he can walk around the bottom of the cage to his heart's content. The bird will be happy and so will your neighbors. Say, how close do your neighbors live?"

"Too close," answered Teach, "Too close."

"So how much is all of this?" asked Preach.

"The twenty-five-pound bag of Turbo Rooster will run you one hundred dollars, the chicken coop will run you $229.00, and with tax, that will come to $352.03. How would you like to pay for that?"

"We've got to split the expense," Teach said to Amos, "I'm going to pay my share as well," said Preach. "You don't have to," replied Teach. "No, I insist, I've kind of taken a liking to the little fellow."

As the four left the feed store, Amos uttered the words, "A ripped rooster, we gonna have one fine fightin bird, he gonna be ripped!"

Chapter Fifteen:
THE TRIP BACK

They waited at the bus stop on U.S. 1, waiting for bus 35 North, the twenty-five-pound bag of Turbo Rooster Brand Feed lashed to the back of Amo's wheelchair, the box with the coop sitting next to Teach and Flathead.

"So, what happened to Delorean?"

"Well, they had him by the so-called private parts," answered Preach. "You mean the balls," said Amos, "Testicles," responded Teach. "There he goes again, correctin my grammar." They all chuckled.

"Whatever they had him by, they had him good, there was an informant, tape recorded telephone calls, banks to launder the dirty money and a suitcase full of cocaine. 'Good as gold,' he called it, 'Good as gold.'"

"So he went to jail, right?" asked Flathead.

"What he did," Preach replied, "was just hire the best lawyer that money could buy. He argued that it was a 'fictitious crime,' and that the government informant had 'set him up.'"

"But how could he argue that he was innocent? Wasn't he caught with a suitcase full of cocaine? 'Good as gold?'" asked Flathead

"He was found 'Not Guilty,' answered Preach, 'Not Guilty.'"

"You see," said Preach, "there's a different justice system for the rich than there is for the poor, but in the end, justice will prevail. For whatever a man soweth, he shall also reap."

"Damn straight," responded Amos.

"Damn straight," echoed Teach.

They boarded the northbound bus, and sat near the back. It sped off toward the restaurant.

"We were left poor and destitute. Me dad scrambled to do anything he could do to make ends meet, and I worked odd jobs, selling newspapers on the street, washing dishes, anything to help with the household expenses.

"Mom says to me, 'Patrick, there's a future for you out there, you're gonna be a shining star, and I love you more than words can tell.'"

"So, I tells me mom, 'Mom,' I says, 'I met a man from the United States Army, he said that I had a great future. He was standing near a sign that said, 'Be All You Can Be,'" "Mom, I've joined the Army."

"Oh son," she says, "Lord protect you, I'll pray for you every day and every night."

"'Mom,' I says, "Not to worry, the world's at peace. Little did I know."

"The military was a lot of drudgery, but things were okay, so I signed up for a second four-year term of enlistment. Things were soon to change."

"I had never heard of a man called Saddam Hussein, but in the summer of 1990 this man decided that he liked the oil fields his neighbor had to the East. He sent one- hundred-thousand Iraqi troops to invade this neighbor country, Kuwait."

"I didn't know much about Kuwait or Iraq, but I knew we were at war when they shipped us out to Saudi Arabia. They called it 'Desert Storm.'"

"When we got there, they had us preparing for an invasion. We were going to 'liberate Kuwait, and free Iraq of despotism.'" "They said that we had to be ready to face the enemy."

"Every once in a while, a Scud Missile or something like that would be thrown in our direction, I lost a couple of friends."

"Then there came the day in late February that they gave us the green light. My unit was given a support role with the M-1 tanks, they'd plow on ahead and we'd do the mop up work."

"The tanks were making good progress, and we were taking in a lot of prisoners. Me friend made a mistake when he walked onto the sand to tell a couple of surrendering Iraqis where to turn themselves in. I screamed 'No!' 'Don't Go There!'" "The poor lad walked right into a minefield."

"He lay there dying, and I couldn't let that happen, so I ran to him. He tried to warn me, but I stepped on another one of those little bastards, cost me my right leg."

"As I lay there bleeding, next to my dying friend, I made a promise to God. I said 'God,' if you deliver me, I will devote my life to your service.'"

All three listened glumly.

"You know that the army challenged me to 'Be all that you can be,' but I ain't even all that I used to be." Preach looked down at his missing leg.

"You sure ain't," said Amos, looking at Preach's artificial leg, "You sure ain't."

"We're almost here," said Teach, as he pressed the black strip which actuated the bell.

"Let's eat lunch," said Amos, "I'm kind of hungry." "Me too," responded Preach, "I'll finish the story after we eat."

They sat down at Smokey's Barbecue and ordered beef sandwiches, French fries, corn on the cob and coleslaw. "Be sure to bring to the table a couple jars of your famous barbecue sauce," Teach asked the waitress, "best barbecue sauce in the world."

Chapter Sixteen:
All Saint's Church of the Holy Deliverer

"So, they discharged me from the army and I became a man of the cloth."

"You know that I was in the army for a time, too," said Flathead, "In that second Gulf War." All three looked at him with surprise, this being the first time he ever mentioned anything about his past life.

"Why don't you tell us about it?" asked Amos, "it could be cath, cath," "Cathartic," responded Teach, finishing Amos's sentence. Amos looked at Teach snidely.

"No," replied Flathead, "I'd much rather listen to you," he looked at Preach.

The food came and they plowed in. After finishing most of the meal, Preach continued with his story.

"I became connected with the All Saint's Church Of The Holy Deliverer. I was interested in evangelism, you know, spreading the Gospel, and I became an assistant priest. They said that they were 'interested in the same,' but I never saw em do much of anything."

The pastor would teach class, mainly to children, but they never really went out and spread the word, 'Someday we'll go out there and do the Lord's work,' he used to say."

"It never seemed to happen, and I began to refer to the church as the All Saint's Church Of The Holy Procrastinator."

"On Saturdays, we would have confessional. One Saturday, something surprising happened, the senior pastor entered the confessional booth."

"He didn't tell me who he was, but I recognized his voice immediately. "I've done something horrible, something reprehensible, and I want to confess my sins," he said. "Confess your sins," I replied, "and you will be saved."

"I've done something that I'm not proud of," he responded, "I did it with a young man in choir practice."

"Say No More, You Low Life Bastard! I screamed to his surprise," "You'll be rottin in Hell for a Long Time!"

"Then I got up and left, right there and then, just left the booth and left the Church. Never went back."

"I was now a member of the Church of The Fresh Air And Blue Sky."

"If I was going to minister to sex offenders, I figured that I might as well go where they were living, under the Julia Tuttle Causeway, near Northwest 36th Street."

"Is that where you met Teach?" asked Flathead.

"We've finished eating and it's time to head back on the Metrorail," said Preach.

They left Smokey's and walked North to the Metrorail Station, Amos, in his wheelchair, with the bag of Turbo Rooster Feed secured to the back the wheelchair's seat, and Flathead, now carrying the box marked "chicken coop." They paid for their tickets and took an elevator up to the departure level.

After a few minutes, they boarded the Northbound Train, and settled in for their trip back home.

"Why don't you finish your story," Preach looked at Teach, "I've been talking way too long as it is."

"I was in three different federal prisons during my time in custody, close to ten years," responded Teach, "they send you to these prisons located in small towns that have hit hard times. First, I was sent to FCI Bennettsville in South Carolina, a little town that hadn't made any social or economic progress since the days when cotton was king, in the mid 1800's.

"But with powerful Southern politicians, they managed to place a prison in that small town. These prisons bring in jobs and revive the economy there are more prisoners in America today than there are farmers and all of these small towns clamor for placement of these prisons to bring in jobs and federal money."

"It's like they build a cage and they stock that cage with animals. Only they're not animals, they're real human beings."

"Social welfare at the expense of human bondage," lamented Preach, "how pitiful is the state of human existence."

"They sent me to two more prisons before they released me, one in Jesup Georgia, and the last one in Coleman, Florida." "A spread the wealth plan," said Amos, "why hog all the money?"

"When they let me go from prison, they put me on something called 'supervised release.' My case was transferred to Miami, where my supervised release officer informed me of the rules that I had to follow.

"There were specific rules relating to sex offenders and where they could live, in Miami, you cannot live within two thousand five hundred feet of parks, bus stops or homeless shelters. There was only one place in Miami that met that description, The Julia Tuttle Sex Offender Colony."

"That be the bridge near Northwest Thirty-Six Street," said Amos

"Actually, under the bridge on Northwest Thirty-Six Street," responded Teach.

"I was forced to live under the bridge with all of these people, thrown together in some kind of melange of sex crazed maniacs, psychopathic lunatics and dysfunctional refugees from the human race. It was there that I met Preach."

"To be clear, I wasn't one of those sex crazed maniacs," said Preach, "I was there to save them. See, God sends you where you can do the most good."

"That's for sure," replied Teach, "Do you remember the funeral."

"You mean the burial at sea?" asked Preach, "What a fine service it was."

"This young man who'd been living in the colony killed another man when he tried to attack him," said Teach, "'I can't go to prison,'" he cried, "'I'm going to die in prison if they arrest me.'"

"So, the residents of the bridge did a little surgery on the dead man, cut off his arms, legs and head, and threw his remains into the bay.

"I needed to get the hell away from there, Preach agreed with me, so both of us packed our belongings and headed south to the MacArthur Causeway, and that's where I met Amos."

"Now we three be a team," responded Amos, "Preach, Teach and Amos, we be great team," he said as he smiled.

"Don't forget Flathead," said Teach, "he's a member as well."

"Yeah, that be right," answered Amos, "he be an auxiliary member."

CHAPTER SEVENTEEN:

ANXIOUS FOR BREAKFAST

The next morning Teach was ready to get going fast and early. "Why are you so anxious for breakfast?" asked Preach, "I thought that you didn't like the way that they mixed the food."

"It ain't be food he be thinking about," replied Amos, "he be thinking about other things."

"Hey," said Teach, "just because I want an early breakfast doesn't mean that I'm after that social worker girl. Besides, I've kind of taken a liking to scrambled eggs and bean curd."

"How you doing little Al?" asked Preach to the Flarry Eyed Grey, now happily ensconced in his perch, "You're a find specimen of a bird, a fine specimen."

"Oh yeah he be," responded Amos, "he be a fine specimen."

"Make sure that he gets his cup of turbo rooster before we leave," said Teach, "He seems to like it."

"Yeah, he be eatin like a champ," replied Amos, "eatin like a champ."

All four headed off for their morning meal.

After the two-mile walk, Teach, Preach, Amos and Flathead reached the entrance to the Christian House of Charity.

"Sir," asked the serving lady, "what can I get for you?" "Sir?" "Oh his head be in the clouds," answered Amos, "He be looking for that Debra lady."

Esmerelda raised her eyebrows as the rest of them chuckled. "She's talking to a man in the back row," replied the serving lady, "Thanks," responded Teach, as he walked toward where she was speaking and sat himself down on her other side.

"Looks like we're gonna be eating alone," said Preach. "Yeah," replied Amos, "looks like that be the case."

"I'm sorry if I was too forward with you yesterday," said Teach to Debra, "Sometimes I make a fool of myself."

"Oh, I thought it was cute," she replied, "you aren't the first guy who tried to flirt with me." "Oh, there are others?" he asked. "No, nothing serious."

"Looks like Teach and that social worker lady are having a serious discussion," said Preach. "Sure do," replied Amos, "Sure do."

"Now tell me about yourself," asked Debra, "What is it that put you out on the street?"

"It's a long sad story, and I know your time is short," answered Teach, "but it started with a pack of cigarettes."

"A pack of cigarettes?" replied the social worker as her ears perked up.

"I tried to get a pack of cigarettes away from a lying girl, she screamed 'rape,' and I went to jail, lost my job, my reputation, and all that I had done to earn me 'Teacher of The Year.'"

"So let me get this straight," said Debra, "All you did was try and get a pack of cigarettes away from this loud-mouthed girl and as a result, you ended up losing your wife, your family, your job and your freedom?"

"That's right," answered Teach, "everything that I worked for my entire life went down the tubes."

"How sad," responded Debra, "you'd think that they had better things to do than to destroy people's lives, and on lies and crazy evidence."

"That's just the thing," said Teach, "The DNA test they me gave came up positive. According to the scientist at the F.B.I crime lab, there was a one in a billion chance that anyone other than myself had had a sexual relationship with that girl."

"Where was that crime lab?" asked the social worker, "I don't remember, somewhere in Kentucky, why do you ask?" replied Teach

"I don't know," responded the social worker, "just curious."

Teach looked over at his friends. "Breakfast is getting cold, I'd better get back with my buddies," he said to Debra, "besides, you probably wouldn't want to be associated with someone who has my kind of baggage."

"I don't know about that," she responded, "You're a very interesting person." They shook hands and Teach took his place back at the table with his friends.

"Whooee!" said Amos, "You and that social worker girl got a thing going!"

"No," said Teach, "we're just friends, just friends."

"Say," who drank my orange juice?" asked Teach

"Sorry, it was me," answered Flathead, "I'll go and get you another." "He's a growing boy," replied Preach, "besides we never figured you were coming back!"

With breakfast finished, the four started their train back to the bridge.

Chapter Eighteen:

Varumpt Varumpt Varumpt Screech!

February 6th, 2010 was a miserable day in Miami for anyone living in that city, much less those residing under a bridge, there was a cold front arriving and the weather had turned windy and rainy. The skies were dark and peppered with rain clouds.

Residents of the bridge community huddled together as the wind ripped through their small living area under the bridge, waves from the bay lapped over rocks that marked the edge of where the sand spit met the bay. It was near impossible to keep warm or dry as lightning danced across the sky, coupled with thunder claps.

"Tis a fine Miami day," said Preach, "the Lord is sending us a message."

"Maybe that message be to get the hell out of here and find us some shelter indoors?" replied Amos.

"We could head over to the Main Library on Flagler Street," answered Teach, "maybe bury our heads in some good books."

"Look at those waves," said Preach, "maybe it's time to head on our way. It's ten o'clock and the library should be open."

"Hey Flathead," asked Teach, "you coming with us to the library?"

"Yeah," answered Flathead, "give me second, I need to take a whiz in the bay."

As Flathead walked over to the rocks near the edge of their small sandy abode where the waters of the bay meet the spit, he could hear the cars thunder overhead.

"Varumpt," "Varumpt," "Varumpt," "Varumpt." "I wonder who would be out driving on a miserable day like today," thought Flathead, as he unzipped his camouflage-colored pants.

Then something caught his attention, something that was different from the ceaseless "Varumpt" "Varumpt" sound that emanated from overhead.

It started the same, "Varumpt," "Varumpt," "Varumpt," but ended with "SCREEEEECH!"

All bridge dweller eyes looked upward when the next noise, a loud BANG assaulted their ear-ways. All of a sudden, the top of a white sedan appeared as if a toy, carelessly thrown into the air by a young child bored of his playtime. The bridge residents watched as the car summersaulted into the water, end over end, finally entering the water at a forty-five-degree angle.

"Holy Mother Mary," screamed Preach, "look at that!"

"There's a woman in that car!" said Flathead, "someone's got to save her."

"Listen," said Teach, "look at the waves and the current, if you head out into those waters you're just going to die along with that lady."

As the car began slipping under the water, Flathead made a major announcement, an announcement that would have a dramatic effect upon the lives of the occupants of the car as well as his own life, "I'm going in to save her!" and with those words, Flathead jumped into the water and with graceful and powerful strokes made his way to where the now completely submerged car had been.

Upon reaching the point of impact, he dove downward under the rough water and grabbed driver's side door handle. He could see a woman inside, screaming and banging on the window. She pointed to the back seat where

The Cockfight

Flathead could see a pink infant safety seat with a young child strapped in.

Flathead reached into his pants pocket and pulled out a military style bowie knife with a metal butt handle. Grabbing the knife backward he used all of his strength to smack the driver's side window with the butt of the knife, the window cracked and as the air escaped, he dragged the woman out of the car and to the surface.

"My Baby, My Baby!" she screamed, "You've got to save my little girl!" "I won't let her drown," replied Flathead," as he swam the hysterical mother to the shore and into the arms of the other bridge dwellers who pulled her out of the water."

"I'm going back," said Flathead.

"You can't go back," loudly spoke Teach, over the sound of the wind and rain, "you'll drown!" "I've got to go back, there's a baby in the car." He turned around in the water and with strong and steady strokes headed back out to where the car had first made impact.

"He'll never make it," said Teach, "the water is fifty feet deep down there."

"Don't ever make pronouncements," replied Preach, "sometimes God has plans that seem farfetched from our simple uneducated human point of view."

As the bridge dwellers watched, Flathead made it to the spot where the car sank, and once again dove into the deep water.

"He's got to save my baby!" screamed the mother, "please God, let him save my baby!"

"He's been down there about a minute," observed Ebenezer, "that's a long time."

"I have faith," replied Preach, "he'll come through."

Immediately thereafter, Flathead exploded to the surface holding with his right arm a scared but very alive baby girl.

As Flathead neared the shore the sirens of emergency rescue vehicles could be heard closing in on the vicinity of the disaster."

"My baby, My baby!" screamed the mother, "You saved my baby!" Teach reached into the water and pulled out the crying infant, next, Preach and Ebenezezer assisted Flathead up to the shore."

"This be great, this be great!" said Amos, "Preach done call Teach 'simple and uneducated,' and he be right, he be right! This be a great day, a great day!"

Chapter Nineteen:
A Real American Hero

"Don't take my picture, please don't take my picture," Flathead pleaded to the newsman, sporting a camera and large flash attachment, but soon, like ants to a picnic, more and more arrived.

The blinding light of the large and powerful flashes of light came from all directions. Flathead tried to hide his face.

"I've got to get out of here," he stated to the others, "I've got to leave."

"But you're a hero, my boy," said Preach, "a hero."

"Look," responded Flathead, "I can't be around here, I don't want to be a hero and I don't need any thanks," he quickly ran off pushing through the crowd of reporters and spectators.

The grateful woman, holding her child, pointed in the direction that Flathead had been but seemed perplexed at his disappearance.

A reporter walked over to Teach, "Do you know who that man was, the one who rescued the woman and her baby?" "All I know," said Teach, "is that he went by the name of 'Flathead.'" "There's one other thing I know, that he's a real hero."

As the day lingered on, other newsmen and reporters descended upon the area. Once in a while a police officer or detective would show up and ask questions to the bridge dwellers.

Ebenezer could be seen mimicking Flathead's stroke as he described the rescue to several official looking men.

"I wonder where Flathead be?" asked Amos, "It's getting late in the day and nobody seen no sight of him."

As the day wore on, and night finally arrived, Preach, Teach and Amos' worry increased, almost as quickly as the news coverage concerning the day's events.

"BREAKING NEWS," barked the words of the newscaster from the television hanging in the corner of Saint Maria's Home For The Destitute, where Preach, Teach and Amos sat down for dinner, "Mystery Man Saves Woman And Child From Certain Death!"

"In an incredible act of courage and bravery, a mystery man couldn't sit by when he watched a car drive off of the Douglas MacArthur Causeway. Witnesses say that he dived into the rough waters not once, but twice in order to save a drowning woman and her child from their sinking car and certain death."

"Yes, He saved my life, and the life of my child," replied the woman to the television interviewer, "If it wasn't for him, neither of us would be alive." A picture flashed on the screen of Flathead, being only partially successful in an attempt to hide his face.

"Who is this man?" asked the newscaster, "Nobody seems to know." "He didn't seem to want the publicity," said an on the scene television reporter, "he just melted into the crowd."

"I think he just got a little nervous," said Preach, "probably didn't want the publicity." "I can understand that," replied Teach, "No matter what you think about freedom of the press, when is the last time you ever saw a news reporter tell the truth." "Amen," responded Amos.

"It's getting late and we'd better head back," said Teach, "things have probably settled down under the bridge. Flathead should also be back, he left all his things, his knapsack and sleeping bag."

The three began their train back to the bridge, "Still not back?" Teach asked Ebenezer, "Still not back," was the response.

Morning came around and so did evening, morning and then evening. "If he's not back by tomorrow morning, I'm going to look through his things," said Teach, "maybe we can find something out about him." "Maybe he's got some relatives who know where we can get ahold of him," responded Preach.

The third morning rolled around and Teach asked Amos if he had "taken care of Al?" "Yeah, he ate like a champ," responded Amos. "Well, I guess we had better take a look at Flathead's knapsack."

Preach, Amos, Ebenezer and One Lip gathered around the abandoned knapsack, and as Teach lifted it up to find an opening a five starred metal object, connected to a red, white and blue ribbon, fell out of a front pocket.

"Will you look at that," said Amos, "if that ain't a fine piece of jewelry." "That's not just a fine piece of jewelry," replied Preach, "that's a Silver Star. They don't give those out like popcorn," he continued, "that's an award for 'Gallantry in Action.'"

"There's another one in here," Teach stated, as he pulled another heavy medallion from the knapsack's pocket, this, a heart shaped one connected to a purple ribbon. The likeness of George Washington was embossed on the front with the words 'For Military Merit' embossed on the back.

"That one there is a 'Purple Heart,'" said Preach, "you don't just earn one of them, you get that from being wounded in action."

"There's a newspaper article and a letter in here as well. I'll read the article out loud," said Teach.

"Swainsville Man Awarded Silver Star"

"A North Carolina man has been awarded the Silver Star for gallantry in action. William Smith, a twenty-year old resident of Swainsville, is the proud recipient of a Silver Star. Awarded for gallantry in action, Mr. Smith is credited for saving seven of his fellow soldiers from certain death when under blistering fire he singlehandedly silenced a machine gun nest while his fellow marines were pinned down and he himself was wounded in the right shoulder."

"Although he could not use his good right arm, he carefully crept from his point of relative safety, bullets whizzing around him. With his left arm holding his rifle, he picked off the three of the enemy who were manning the gun. When the other Iraqis saw what happened, they commenced running away. In a ceremony attended by important people, including Brigadier General Michael Kelley, who personally pinned the medal on Mr. Smith, he called Mr. Smith, 'A Real American Hero.'"

"If that don't beat all," said Amos, "this boy be a real American Hero.'" "Wow," was the only response the onlookers could mutter." "If that ain't some kind of story," said Ebenezer.

"There's another letter here," replied Teach, "this one from a lawyer."

"March 18th, 2009
"Dear Mr. Smith,
"I hope that this letter finds you well. As you are aware, your court date is scheduled for April the 8th. We have discussed your case at length as well as your possible defenses concerning felony possession of one and a half ounces of marijuana.

"As you are aware, this will make your third felony arrest for possession of pot, and that you are now facing an enhanced penalty as a 'Habitual Offender,' Under North Carolina Law, the District Attorney can seek one hundred and twenty-five months of incarceration. If you are willing to plead guilty, he will recommend only one hundred months.

"I am aware of your defenses, the fact that each prior arrest concerned only 'one and a half ounces of pot.'" "I am also aware of the fact that you suffer from 'post-traumatic stress disorder' and "require the pot to relieve the constant pain you suffer from your shoulder wound."

"However, possession of one and a half ounces of marijuana is a Level

The Cockfight

I Felony in the State of North Carolina. Since this is your third arrest and you were caught red handed, you face sentencing as a 'Habitual Felony Offender.'" "I find your explanation wanting and feel that you have no real defense to put forth in this matter. Therefore, I recommend that you accept the offer of the Assistant District Attorney."

"Holy jumping Jesus," said Amos, "Is they wantin to put Flathead in jail for one hundred months for possessin what amounts to a few joints?" "That seems to be the long and the short of it," responded Teach.

"But ain't North Carolina in the bible belt, Preach?" asked Amos, "Ain't they supposed to be Christians?" "Oh, don't you see," replied Preach, "many of those bible belt folks pray like Christians, but sin like the devil."

Chapter Twenty:
One Fine Rooster

"That's one fine rooster you've got there," said El Cabron, "give him a few more months, and a bird like that has the makings of a champion. How much do you want for him?"

"Al Capone is not for sale," responded Teach, "Not for any price." El Cabron took a wad of twenties out of his wallet. "Ah come on," he continued, "everyone has a price, how about a thousand dollars?"

"Listen to the man," replied Amos, "he's not for sale, no price no how." "Oh well," responded El Cabron, "at least I tried."

"Tonight's first fight," said the man with hat and tickets stuffed into the band, "Number Thirteen versus Number Eight."

"That be the brown bird," said Amos, "this gonna be a great fight. I'm putting my money on the Number Thirteen, seeing the way he put that other bird away last fight." "Guess I will too," replied Teach, "too bad Flathead isn't around to see the match."

"What's it been?" asked Preach, "over two weeks?" "Sounds about right," replied Teach, "I hope that kid is okay." "Me too," responded Preach, "me too."

"Last call for bets, last call," said the man with the hat. "I'll put a hundred on that Thirteen bird," said Amos to the man. "Me as well," added Teach.

A loud "clap" emanated from the bell and the match was on. Both roosters went after each other immediately, wings fluttering, legs kicking. After less than a minute, Number Eight's right leg spur came up and sliced into the 'Brown Bomber's' left wing. Blood began to spurt as the Number Thirteen writhed in pain. Less than twenty seconds later, he lay dead in the center of the cockpit.

"Well, there go our bird," mourned Amos. "And there goes our money," replied Teach.

As the next round was getting set up, Preach walked back over to Teach, "So did you speak to that Debra girl, the social worker, maybe she'll have some news about where Flathead is?"

"She said that she tried to talk to him when she first met him, but that he didn't want to tell her anything about himself. She said that she'd ask around and if she found out about anything that she'd let me know," responded Teach.

"Well, that's better than nothing," said Preach, "we'll just have to pray that the boy's okay."

"Hey Teach," asked Amos, 'they getting ready for the next round, ain't you betting?" "Sorry Preach," said Teach, as he left to find the man with the hat, raising two fingers to place his wager.

Two hours quickly passed and Teach asked Amos "how he was doing?" "I ain't won a single match," responded Amos, "not a single damn match, and I'm running out of money quicker than shit through a goose." "You mean through a rooster," responded Teach, "a rooster." "I ain't even gonna comment on that one."

"Taking bets for the final match!" screamed the man, "Taking bets for the final match." "Who's fightin?" asked Amos. "Number Thirty-Four versus Forty-Seven."

"I've seen that Forty-Seven, said Amos, I call him Lemon Peeler. He be that yellow legged hatch that tore half the skin offn that ornery black bird a few months back. I'm putting my money on that bird." "I don't know," responded Teach, "Thirty-Four is a pretty tough bird, he might come out on top." "Take my word," replied Amos, "I know both these birds and Lemon Peeler gonna demolish old Rojo Alabama."

"Last call for bets, last call for bets!" screamed the bet taker. "I'll put two hundred on Number Forty-Seven," said Amos. "Me too," responded Teach.

The sound of the bell reverberated off of bridge, as the roosters went right at each other. As they flailed their feet and wings at each other, it was almost impossible to tell which one was winning the match.

Then, after about two minutes, Rojo sliced into the Lemon Hatch's left leg. The gamecock fell to the floor of the pit, writhing in pain. Seeing his opportunity, Rojo demolished the other bird, finishing him off with a furious burst of flailing wings, feet and sharpened spurs.

"Well, there goes the money," rued Amos, "Easy come easy go," responded Teach.

El Cabron approached and spoke, "I'll offer you twelve hundred and fifty dollars for the Flarry Eyed Grey." "He's still not for sale repeated Teach, not at any price." "That's right," added Amos, "still aint for sale, no price, no how."

As the sun rose the next morning, all three headed out to the Christian House of Charity.

"Have you heard anything about Flathead?" Teach asked Debra, as he sat down next to her.

"Nothing yet," she responded, "but I understand that a lot of people are looking for him. They've sent out a flyer to all of the government offices, a BOLO. 'Be on the lookout for William Smith, may be armed and dangerous, If you encounter this man, do not approach, but call the authorities immediately.'"

"Holy Mother Mary," responded Preach, as he listened to their conversation, "we've got to do some praying for this boy. We need to pray that they find him and that they don't harm him."

Chapter Twenty-one:

Prayers Answered

"I'd like to learn a little more about your friend," said Debra, "and a little more about you." "Why don't we meet for dinner?" Teach suggested, "there's a little restaurant at Seaside that has great Cuban cuisine, it's called the Cuban American Café and they have the best arroz con pollo. Why don't we meet there at seven p.m.?"

"Sounds great, I look forward to seeing you then," she replied

"Holy Macamoli, looks like Teach got himself a date," crowed Amos, "and she ain't too bad lookin either!"

"It's not so much a date as it is an investigative conference," responded Teach, "she wants to know about Flathead and he is my major concern. I'm not exactly living the high life, sleeping under a bridge and all, and I doubt that she'd be interested in someone with my background and my baggage."

"Don't be too hard on yourself," said Preach, "with God, all things are possible."

"You got that right," responded Amos, glancing at the good-looking social worker, "you got that right."

Breakfast finished, the three headed back toward the bridge. Teach stopped to purchase flowers from a street vendor. "That will be twenty- five dollars said the Flower Lady." As he counted his money he looked at Preach and Amos, "Moneys running out," said Teach, "I've got less than a hundred dollars left."

"Let me help you with the flowers," said Preach, "seeing that it's your first date and all." "It's not a date," protested Teach. "Ain't no matter," chimed Amos, "I want in on this too." Preach and Amos paid the bill.

They made their way back to the bridge, and stopped to check on Al Capone. "How you doing little bird?" asked Preach, "You're a fine bird, aren't you?" "He's been eatin real well," replied Amos, "look at how big he's been growing."

"I knew it was a good idea to buy that Turbo Feed," said Teach, "he's going through it like jelly doughnuts. Pretty soon we're going to have to take another trip down south to the feed store, and that's going to cost some money."

"Hadn't you better get spruced up before your meeting with the lady?" replied Preach, "why don't you head over to the men's room at the main library on Flagler Street and get washed up?"

"You know, that's a good idea," responded Teach, "a good idea."

"Say, who be that Flagler guy they named the street after?" Amos asked.

"Oh, him and that Julia Tuttle lady got together to develop Miami." "You mean that sex offender bridge lady?" asked Amos. "Yeah," responded Teach, "He owned the railroad and she owned the sex offender colony, now you can take a train and they'll drop you off right there!"

Teach went on his way.

"Am that true?" Amos asked Preach, "Did that Tuttle lady really own the sex offender colony?" "Lord knows," responded Preach, "but whatever it was she did together with that Flagler man must have certainly been an unholy alliance."

As Teach walked on toward the library, a tune crept into his head. He couldn't quite remember where he first heard it, but it had to do with being poor and living in the wrong part of town.

He whistled and hummed it as he scrubbed his skin raw at the public restroom. Other homeless men watched and smiled as his infectious good mood and singing caught on.

He put on his cleanest clothes and spent a few hours at the library relaxing with a book. He bought lunch at a hotdog cart, next, he went back to Burdock's Department Store where he tracked down the perfume lady.

"Let me have a squirt of the best cologne you have," he asked. and the lady produced a brown bottle with an Italian sounding name. "That smells pretty good," he stated to the lady. "It's our best," she responded, "and it's only three hundred dollars a bottle. Can I wrap one up for you?" "I'll pass on that today," he replied, "but I'll think about it."

"Say, do you know what time it is?" he asked. "It's six thirty," she replied. "I best be on my way," and he headed briskly toward Seaside and the Cuban American Café.

"You smell nice," said Debra, as they met outside of the restaurant, "what is that cologne you're wearing?" "Oh, just something I've found that women like." "What's it called?" asked Debra. "Let's not ask complicated questions," responded Teach, "we're just here to eat dinner and discuss Flathead."

"Waiter! A table with a Bay view," demanded Teach. "Right this way, sir and madam, here is our best table."

Teach pulled out a chair for Debra and both sat down. As Teach looked out toward the bay, he was astounded at the view, most astounding was the fact that if he squinted hard enough, he could actually see his buddies a quarter mile away under the MacArthur Causeway.

"So where exactly do you live?" asked Debra. "Well, I'm sort of unsettled right now," answered Teach, living from place to place." As he spoke some kind of altercation broke out under the bridge and you could vaguely see two men loudly gesturing at each other."

"So, what can I get you?" asked the waiter, "Some wine?" "Yes, that sounds great," answered Teach, "What do you recommend?"

"Listen," said Debra, "you don't have to." "No, I insist," responded Teach, "It's my treat."

"So, tell me all about yourself, Rick."

"Well Debra, what do you want to know?"

"I want to know who you are? Where you're from? and where you're going?" She gazed into his eyes.

"I've already told you how I lost everything."

"I want to know who Rick Bradford really is, and I want hear it again, the whole story, and I want you to look into my eyes when you tell it." She reached over and clasped his hand.

"Are you sure you want to hear the entire story?" he asked. "I'm sure," was the response, "Very sure."

Time passed as he related the whole sorry story to her.

"So, you really were 'Teacher of The Year' and this isn't some kind of crazy tale?" "That's right," he responded. "You lost your job, your wife, your family and your freedom because a lying fourteen-year-old girl screamed 'rape?'"

"That's the long and the short of it," he replied, "that, and a so-called positive DNA test." Tears came down her right cheek as she grabbed his arm. Just then, Preach and Amos showed up at their table.

"What are you guy's doing here?" asked Teach

"Oh, we just came to see how you're getting along?" answered Preach. "You know this man be the greatest guy I know," Amos chimed as he looked at Debra, "but he sure do a lot a grammar correctin." They all laughed.

Chapter Twenty-two:

The Lord's Mercy

As all four sat at the table as the conversation turned to Flathead. "You know, he be a real American hero," said Amos, "he be saving all those fellow Marines and then he be saving that lady and her car that done fell into the water."

"We're all concerned about the boy," responded Preach, "it's now been over three weeks and no one's seen hide seen nor tail of him."

"It all seems so sad, so crazy," said Debra, "they say that he's 'armed and dangerous,' but it sounds to me like he wouldn't hurt a fly."

"That's because the lady he saved told them how he used his military knife to break through the window," responded Teach, "they turned it around to make it look like he attacked her with the knife. The truth always takes second place when a lie will do."

"Amen," replied Preach

"Me too," added Amos.

"Here's your check," said the waiter. "It's a good thing that you guys came when you did," Teach whispered to Preach and Amos, "I might need a little money to help with the bill." "That's what friends are for," whispered Preach back."

"I overheard what you said, and you're not paying a penny," responded Debra, "I'm paying this one, and I insist." "You really don't have to," replied Teach. "No," she countered, "I insist."

The next morning all three woke up early and Preach filled Al Capone's food bowl with the last remaining feed in the bag. All three admired the now nearly mature bird. "Boy, ain't she something," said Amos, "she about the best gamecock there is." "No doubt about that," responded Teach, "No doubt about that."

"Don't throw out that empty feed bag," Amos asked Preach, "gonna make a nice seat cover for my chair."

The three commenced their walk down northeast second avenue toward the Christian House of Charity, Amo's wheelchair now sporting a "Turbo Rooster" seat cover. When they joined the morning line of breakfast seekers, they knew something was up when Debra briskly walked over to the three.

"They've got Flathead, he's at the Miami-Dade County Jail." "Lord's Mercy," responded Preach," Is the boy okay? "I understand that he is," responded Debra, "it's been all over the news, stories like 'Dangerous Felon Captured After Three Weeks On The Run.'"

"Apparently, he walked the Causeway over to Miami Beach. He was sleeping out near the Versace Mansion on Ocean Drive, and someone recognized him and told the police. He was arrested 'without a struggle' according to the news," said Debra.

"Since I'm a social worker, they'll let me go in and see him. He has to authorize visitors, and I'll make sure that he puts you three on his visitation list."

"Today is Thursday," responded Preach, "I think they have visiting hours in the early evening, why don't we head south to the feed store to pick up some food for Al? When we come back, we'll visit Flathead at that ten story Tower of Hell."

"We're kind of short on funds," said Teach, "we may have hit the road and pick up some money. We're gonna have to get off a few stops early, there's a

The Cockfight

good place where Sunset Drive meets U.S. 1. Do we have any signs with us?"

"Sure do," replied Amos, "I always keep them here under my seat."

All three headed toward the Metrorail Station. It wasn't long before they heard the words, "Stand Back, Stand Back, A South Bound Train Approaching."

The three boarded the train and they soon found themselves at the Sunset Drive Station. "Time to get off," said Teach, "let me have my sign."

Amos reached under his seat. The sign that Teach held was made of cardboard. Words in large black magic marker read, "WILL WORK FOR FOOD." "Here's your sign, Preach," said Amos. It had a small cross on the upper left and read, "WILL PRAY FOR YOUR SOUL, DONATIONS ACCEPTED." "Where's your sign, Amos?" asked Teach. "Here it be," responded Amos, "WOUNDED IN ACTION."

All three exited the train and soon found themselves at the busy intersection where the two roads met, and it didn't take long for donations to come pouring in.

"Hey Preacher Man," said a lady in an expensive European car, "would you pray for my ingrown toe nail?" "Course I will," and he reached through the car window and touched the lady's left shoulder, "May the lord heal this lady's toe, and make her toe as good as new." She took a hundred dollar bill out of her purse and gave it to Preach.

But of all those who garnered the most sympathy, Amos was far ahead of the rest. "Injured in action," asked one man, "and look at how the government has treated you! Say buddy, where were you wounded? In Vietnam?"

Amos learned always to agree with whatever it was that the person alluded to, "Yep, in Nam," he responded. "Say," asked the man, "I was in Vietnam, where in Vietnam were you hit?" Amos always pointed to the traffic light, usually now green, "Say, you best be on your way fore those cars behind you start honking," he would say. Invariably the person in the car would push a twenty in his direction and head off.

"Where in Nam were you hit?" Teach would joke, "how about Thirty-Six

Street and Biscayne Boulevard!" With that, Teach and Amos would crack up laughing.

Once in a while, a police car would come by and warn the three "not to interfere with traffic." After the second of these warnings, they decided to head off on their way.

"What be our take for the day," asked Amos, as Preach and him handed over their largesse to Teach. "Three hundred and thirty-six dollars and fifty-seven cents," responded Teach, "here are your shares."

They walked back to the station, and made their way south toward the bus stop and feed store.

"How's that feed working?" asked the man at the store, I'll bet it's doing pretty well seeing that you decorated the chair with the empty bag." "Yeah, it seems to be working," replied Amos, "we'll take another." The man retrieved a ten lb. bag and placed it on the counter.

"And how's that cage working, the one that's supposed to turn off the rooster morning alarm clock?" "Oh, that be working real well too," Amos responded, "we ain't had no death threats since." They all chuckled and after that departed for their appointment with Flathead.

Chapter Twenty-three:

Ten Stories of Hell

The Miami-Dade County Jail was built in 1961. It is a ten-story building connected by a bridge to the back of the Metro Justice Building. It is arguably the ugliest building in a city known for its ugly buildings.

As you walk toward the entrance and glance to the top, you will see barbed wire framing the structure like a crown of thorns. Upon entry into the building, you will be met with green painted walls, of a color which would make any restroom proud.

There is a glass window with a louvered metal curtain, where, if you're lucky, a receptionist guard will great you after ten or fifteen minutes of oppressive waiting in a room that looks like a latrine and smells like one too.

"Can I help you?" asked the guard, Preach leading the way. "Yes," we're here from the Church of the Blue Sky and Fresh Air, and we're here to see a friend." "Can I have your names?"

"I'm Father Patrick O'Malley, this is Rick Bradford and this is Amos, Amos Haveaseat." "That be right," replied Amos. "Let me see your identification," asked the guard. Preach and Teach pushed theirs under the window slot. "What about you, Mr. Haveaseat?" "I done left mine at home." Well, let me check for your name and see if it's on the visiting list." "Hmmm, looks like it is. I'll let you in this time, but make sure to have some ID next time around," said the guard.

As they walked through the metal detector, Teach leaned down to Amos and whispered, "You better pick up a library card next time we're downtown, something with your name on it."

They were led into a main entryway where a holding cell was visible, inside were two drunk and haggardly looking men. A guard window sat on their right, and another across the hall by the holding cell. High powered rifles were clearly visible, attached to the walls of the guard vestibules, keys at the ready.

Preach walked up to an inside booth "We're here to visit Flath . . .," "William Smith," Teach corrected him. "He's on the seventh floor," answered the guard, "the elevator is behind you."

As the three entered the elevator, Preach began explaining, "The higher you go the worst it is. The seventh floor is pretty much where they put murderers, rapists, and those who are an escape risk. At least it's not the ninth floor."

"What's on the ninth floor?" asked Teach. "Oh, that's the psych floor, full of inmates screaming all day and all night, a real party. There are no treatment options in this God forsaken county, so they just pick em up off the street and throw em in here."

"Sounds like a fun place," said Teach. "It ain't be fun," responded Amos, "I've been here. You be lucky cause you been in federal lockup, compared to this place that be like the Ritz."

As the elevator door opened the three men were met by the strong stench of urine. A guard booth in the middle of the floor was manned by two guards, whom they could hardly see through the shaded glass. "We're here to see William Smith," said Preach, hobbling along. Teach followed, pushing Amos and his wheelchair.

The guard pointed to a bank of windows to his left, each window had a two-way phone attached to the wall. "I wonder which window he'll be at?"

asked Teach, "I guess we've got to wait till they bring him out."

Amos loudly proclaimed, "There he be, there he be!" pointing to the third window from the left.

With those words, all three approached the window, they could see a visibly shaken and much changed Flathead. His eyes and cheeks were sunken and it looked as though he had lost twenty pounds. They tried to speak to him through the glass but he pointed to the telephone receiver on the wall.

They crowded around the receiver and through the static, tried to speak and hear Flathead's voice.

"How are you doing hero lad!" spoke Preach in a booming voice, "We've all been praying for you!"

"I ain't been doing too well," Preach, "they want to send me back to North Carolina and they're holding me in this hell hole until my court hearing. They call it an 'Extradition hearing.'"

"When will that take place?" asked Preach.

"SPEAK UP," was the reply through the static.

"WHEN WILL THAT BE?'

"THEY SAY IN A COUPLE OF WEEKS," was the barely audible reply.

"Can you be a little lower with your voice?" asked a guard to Preach.

"We can't hear him over the phone, isn't there a phone that works?" replied Preach.

"Sorry," replied the guard, "that's the way it is."

Preach turned back to the window and continued to try and listen to the visibly shaken man.

"I can't go back, I JUST CAN'T GO BACK, they're gonna put me away for ten years, and now I'm told that they're going to add charges because I'm a fugitive."

"Listen," replied Teach, "whatever happens, you'll get through it. Just remember this one phrase, 'Illigitimi non carborundum.'"

"What that be meaning?" asked Amos.

"IT MEANS, 'DON'T LET THE BASTARDS GRIND YOU DOWN,"

he voiced loudly into the telephone mouthpiece.

"All I did was smoke a little weed to make the pain go away," said Flathead, "If I hadn't been wounded in the shoulder, I never would have even thought about it. My life is over, my life is over . . ." he lamented.

Amos took the receiver from Preach's hand, "Look, your life ain't be over, you just got to pull yourself out of it, you've just got to be makin the best of it. Look at my here legs, my life wasn't over when they shot me in the back. I got a future and I'll be damned if they gonna take that away from me," he let out a broad smile.

"VISITING TIME IS OVER, VISITIING TIME IS OVER, PLEASE PROCEED TO THE EXIT," came a voice over the loudspeaker.

"Look," said Teach, "we'll all come back and visit you." "And we'll all be praying for you," added Preach.

Chapter Twenty-four:

A Systematic Training Program

The next morning rolled around and Teach put food into Al Capone's cup while Amos watched.

"Look," said Amos, "if we be training Al for the big match, we best start takin him out for some exercise."

"You're right," said Teach, "have you got an idea?" "Sure do," replied Amos, "give me a little of that there twine, and help me tie it to my chair." "That's great," said Teach, "that way we can take him along with us for our walks."

Teach affixed some brown twine to the arm of Amo's wheelchair, on the other end, he affixed a slipknot.

Opening up the door of the cage slowly, he tossed the loop over the rooster's head and pulled it tight. Although he fought a little at first, the gamecock was now firmly attached to the rolling chair.

"That's quite a contraption you got there," said Preach, as the three men made their way toward the Christian House of Charity, rooster attached by string, "We're going to be the pride of the breakfast line," went Amos.

"Sorry sir," said the man in charge of the morning breakfast handouts, "you can't take an animal inside, Health Department Rules."

"He ain't no animal, "responded Amos, "he's Al Capone, the finest gamecock there be."

"Sorry," said the man, "not in the eating area."

"Those two can come in," said the man, pointing at Preach and Teach, "and they can bring you your breakfast while you wait outside."

"We'll come back and bring you your food," replied Teach.

As Teach and Preach went inside, several men came by to admire the fine fighting cock. "He ain't no ordinary rooster," Amos told several men as they gathered to look, "he be turbo charged." Amos pointed at the "turbo rooster" feedbag affixed to the back of his wheelchair seat.

Meanwhile, as Teach and Preach waited their turn in the serving line, Debra approached.

"Where's Amos?" she asked, "I've got some really good news for him, we've arranged it so he can get a power chair! But first, he's got to see a psychologist who can confirm that the chair is necessary."

"Ah, that's great," said Preach, "the Lord answers prayers. The boy is sitting right outside with Al Capone, the rooster."

"A rooster!" said Debra, "I've got to see this." She rushed outside to see Amos and the attached rooster, and to give him the good news." "We better follow her," said Teach, as both went out to watch Amos receiving the 'good news.'

"I ain't be needin no psychologist psychiatrist," said Amos, "I be menally balanced and fine!"

"It's only part of the procedure, he needs to analyze you," replied Debra, "his office is on Biscayne Blvd. and Eighteenth Street, just a short walk from here. Just go there and he'll certify that you need a power chair, it'll be as simple as that."

"But I be fine in the mind," Amos protested, "I ain't need no analyzation."

"Your friends can come with you," responded Debra. "Won't you go with him?" Debra looked at Teach and Preach.

"Of course we will," answered Preach, "It'll be like an outing with good friends."

"Great," said Debra, "your appointment is at 1:00 p.m. with Doctor Von Schlumpkin."

"Dr. Von Schmuckin!" Amos repeated, "No," Debra corrected him, "Von Schlumpkin, Von Schlumpkin."

As they left the Christian House of Charity, rooster in tow, Amos was in what best can be described as a rare mood.

"I don't wanna be seeing no fuckin schmuckin," protested Amos in a loud voice. "It's Von Schlumpkin," Teach corrected him.

"OKAY!" Screamed Amos, "YOU DONE CORRECTED ME FOR THE LAST TIME! I AIN'T GONNA SEE NO DOCTOR FUCKIN VON SLUMPKIN EITHER!"

Preach and Teach looked at each other and smiled. Were Amos not taking the matter so seriously, they would probably have burst out laughing.

As they worked their way toward the doctor's office, Amos screamed out loud and at no-one in particular, "THE COMMUNIST REVOLUTION BE COMIN SOON, BEWARE CAUSE THE END OF THE WORLD BE COMIN, THE END OF THE WORLD BE COMIN!"

People watched as the three men and one rooster moved along. It was a long walk, but soon they found themselves in front of an upscale office building a couple of miles north of downtown.

As they entered the building, a guard at the door looked with concern at Amos, who still looked perturbed. "Is he okay?" "Yeah, I be fine," replied Amos, "now that I been analyzed, let's get the hell out of here!"

"There's a little bit more to it than that," responded Teach, "Can you tell us what floor Dr. Von Schlumpkin is?" he asked the security guard.

"Oh yeah, sure, he's on the ninth floor." The three made their way out of the elevator and into what can best be described as an opulent office.

"Can I help you?" asked the receptionist. "Yeah, you can be helpin me," responded Amos, "where be your bathroom, I gotta take a whiz." She pointed to a small door across from her, big enough for Amos, but not for Amos and his wheelchair, rooster attached.

Amos rocketed the chair toward the door, hitting walls on both sides of the door, plaster cascaded off and landed onto the floor. He backed up and repeated this procedure three or four more times, each time the rooster flapped its wings, trying to get away.

"Sir!" yelled the lady. "SEE!" responded Amos, "I DONE NEED A POWER CHAIR, I NEEDS A FUCKIN POWER CHAIR!"

A man in suit and tie exited his office and walked over to the receptionist, quietly asking, "What seems to be the trouble?"

"This man, err, what's your name sir?" "Amos, Amos Haveaseat," "Mr. Haveaseat has a one o:clock appointment."

"Well," said the neatly dressed man, "I'm Dr. Von Schlumpkin, and I'm pleased to meet you," he extended his hand out to Amos, "It's a little early but please come into my office."

"That be great Dr. Von Shumkin," replied Amos, "cause I be wantin to see you too, real bad, real bad."

"Well that's a fine rooster you got there, Mr. what is it? Haveaseat?" "Yeah, he be my friend, he be one of my good friends, them other guys I be with be my friends too, but they think that I done need to see you allin a cause of my needin a power chair."

"So how are you feeling today, Mr. Haveaseat?" "Well tellin you the truth, I be a little aggravated as they tells me I got to be analasized in order to be given one of them chairs, but truth be told is I really need to take a whiz causn I ain't be able to use the bathroom what you have causn it be too small."

"It sounds like you have a little bit of pent-up hostility," responded the doctor.

"Lookie here doctor, I don't need to be told that I got no 'pent up hostility.'"

"Tells you what, Mother Fucker, you wanna see some pent up hostility?

You wanna see some pent up hostility? God Damn It, I JUST WANT A POWER CHAIR. THE COMMUNIST REVOLUTION BE COMIN, IT BE COMIN SOON, THE REVOLUTION BE COMIN SOON!"

"Nurse," calmly spoke the doctor as he picked up his office phone, "Call security."

Chapter Twenty-five:
The Long Walk Back

"Well, it looks like a power chair isn't in the cards today," said Teach. "No," responded Preach, "when security forced us to leave the building, it became apparent to me as well."

"Hey look, I don't need no power chair and I certainly don't need no analyzation, causin you doin a great job pushin me aroun Teach, I ain't got no complaints."

"Yeah," responded Teach, "Do this do that, go here go there, who needs a power chair when this slave here can accomplish the job full time?"

"Just payin the white race back for a little what they done to the black man." They all laughed.

As they made their way back, the rooster started pecking on at a half eaten granola bar sitting on top of an abandoned newspaper. "What's that you're eating," asked Preach to the bird.

As he got closer he could read headlines on the abandoned paper.

"FUGITIVE TO BE CHARGED IN FEDERAL DRUG CONSPIRACY." Let me have this newspaper, little bird, you can keep the rest," said Preach, as the bird continued consuming the granola bar.

"A Dangerous Fugitive Will Be Extradited Back To North Carolina To

Face Federal Drug Conspiracy Charges," Preach read out loud.

"Drug conspiracy charges?" blurted Teach."

"Mr William Smith, who was living under the MacArthur Causeway, was arrested after fleeing the scene of an assault. Armed with a dangerous military attack knife, he thrust it toward a woman and her daughter who shortly before had been traveling across the causeway. He used such force that the car window broke in pieces.

"Next, he dragged the woman and her daughter out of the car and deposited them on a dirty spit of sand under the bridge. If not for the arrival of the authorities, it could have been much worse. Mr. Smith, who fled the scene, was captured hiding out on the beach."

"Attacked a woman wid a knife? Attacked a woman and daughter wid a knife?" said Amos, "what kind of bullshit is this???"

"Let him finish," responded Teach, "what does the rest say?" "It says," Preach continued, "that he's being charged by both the Federal Government and The State of North Carolina with being part of a dangerous drug conspiracy. That he's 'facing life in prison.'"

"This is bullshit, pure bullshit," said Amos. "You got that right," replied Teach

"Oh, responded Preach, this is rare, here is a quote from the woman, 'When I first saw him coming at me, I was scared out of my wits, I screamed for the safety of my baby!'"

"You know," said Preach, "there's a place in Hell for all of these people, the newspaper, the authorities, maybe even the woman, but more likely they just took her words and twisted them around."

"You got that right," replied Teach, "why print the truth when a lie will do? Makes better headlines and sells more newspapers."

"Listen," we've got to go see Flathead," said Preach, "he's probably feelin real low."

"We're almost back to the bridge," said Teach, "let's put Al back in his cage and head on off to the Dade County Jail."

Amos placed Capone in his coop, "Now you be a good bird, we're gonna be back a little late, gotta see a friend who be in a bad situation."

They headed off toward Northwest Twelfth-Street and the ten stories of hell.

"I don't be understanding how they be charging him both federal an by the State a North Carolina, it don't make no sense," said Amos, "an why he be facin life in prison for smoking a few joints for his dramatic stress syndrome?"

"None of this makes sense," replied Teach, "not the charges, not the stories, not the quotes, not the fact that he's a hero but none of this is mentioned. It's like we're living in some kind of alternative universe where everything is backwards from what it's supposed to be."

"Oh, don't you know that that's the way Satan works," said Preach, "he takes things that are good and twists them around to make them look evil, he operates on lies, he is the enemy of the truth."

"You got that right," replied Teach.

"Sure do," responded Amos.

Chapter Twenty-six:
Feeling Low

"My life is over, my life is over," cried Flathead through the inch thick visiting booth glass at the Dade County Jail."

"Your life isn't over," responded Preach, "The Lord has plans, it's just that sometimes we don't know what those plans are," responded Preach.

"Look at this, Look at this," said Flathead, as he pushed a paper against the glass so it could be read by the visitors. Teach leaned close to the glass and read the paper out loud.

"Bill Of Indictment, United States Of America versus William Smith, Julio Rodriquez, Juan Garcia, Manuel Vazquez, Hector Castro, and Joseph White" "Violations; 21 United States Code, Section 841, 21 United States Code Section 846, United States Code Section 848"

COUNT 1

"From in and around March of 2008 and continuing until the present, in Swainsville County, which is in the Mountain District of North Carolina and Elsewhere, these individuals did knowingly and intentionally combine, conspire, confederate and agree with each other and others, both known and unknown to the Grand Jury, to possess with intent to distribute, a quantity of methamphetamine, a Schedule II controlled substance."

1. Said conspiracy involved at least 500 grams of a mixture and substance containing a detectable amount of methamphetamine, in violations of Title 21, United States Code sections 846 and 841(a)(1).

COUNT 2

2. That from in and around March 2008 to the present, the defendants, numbering five or more persons, engaged in a Continuing Criminal Enterprise in violation of Section 848 of Title 21 of the United States Code."

"What it all be meaning?" asked Amos.

"Wait," I'm not finished," responded Flathead, and he pushed another document up to the glass.

This one read "Notice Pursuant To 21 United States Code Section 851." "Pursuant to 21 United States Code Section 851, the United States Government Hereby Gives Notice Of The Following Two Felony Drug Convictions: March 2008, Swainsville, North Carolina Superior Court, and March 2008 Swainsville, North Carolina Superior Court."

"So, what does it all mean?" asked Preach.

"I'll tell you what it means," responded Flathead, "It means that they want to put me in jail for the rest of my life for smoking marijuana!"

"And all in order to stop the pain from the gunshot wound I received after saving my buddies," he hung his head.

"If that don't be shit," said Amos, "If that don't be shit."

"Who are those other people and what is this thing about meth?" asked Teach. "I don't even know who those people are," responded Flathead, "All I know is that I bought an ounce and a half of marijuana from that White guy who runs a 'self-medication' program. I don't know what this guy was into and I don't know a thing about a 'drug conspiracy.'"

"But weren't you already convicted of having the ounce and a half of marijuana before? It sounds like they're trying you for the same crime again, and just throwing in new charges for the same thing," responded Teach, "You plead guilty to two felonies in state court, and now the federal government wants to punish you again for the same act, but call it something else, but it was the same act and you didn't do anything else!"

"I'm not a genius," said Teach, "but I think there's something in the Constitution that prohibits this, something called The Bill of Rights."

"Don't put yourself down," responded Preach, "you're as smart as anyone I've ever met."

"I'm going down to the Main library and do some research," replied Teach, "this just doesn't sound right, trying someone twice for the same thing, and then punishing them even worse for the same act? These two things just don't sound right."

"Please Teach, anything that you can find out would be appreciated," said Flathead, "I'm really depressed, really depressed, I don't know how I'm going live through this? Life in prison, life in prison . . .," Flathead again hung his head on his hands and began to sob.

"The crazy thing," added Flathead, "is that if I had had the money to pay my court appointed attorney, I wouldn't even have had a single felony conviction."

"Come again?" asked Teach. "That's right," answered Flathead, "In North Carolina they make you pay for your court appointed lawyer, even if you don't have the money."

"But isn't that why they appoint you an attorney, because you don't have the money?" asked Teach.

"What happened was that they offered me a plea to a misdemeanor for the two charges but there was a deadline, and in order to take the plea I would have to have had the money to pay my court appointed lawyer. I couldn't raise the money, so they indicted me for the two felonies," he sobbed some more.

"Listen," said Preach, "you've got to keep your spirits up, God loves you, you've just got to do some praying."

"Look, added Teach, "When I'm done with the research, I'll come back and let you know what I've found out. You just keep on keeping on, don't lose hope."

With those words, Teach, Preach and Amos said goodbye to the sullen looking man and left the Dade County Jail.

"Do you think there's something you can do to help Flathead?" asked Preach. "I don't know," responded Teach, "but I'm going to the library and see what I can find out. It all seems so wrong, so wrong."

"You got that right," replied Amos, "You got that right."

"You know," said Preach, I'm really worried about Flathead. You had better get to work on this research as quickly as you can, it sounds like he's caught up in this unholy system and only God can save him now."

The three headed back on their long walk to the bridge.

Chapter Twenty-seven:
An Offer You Cannot Refuse

"You be knowing, Preach, that there be a big fight coming up and there be a lot of money to be made," said Amos

"Cockfighting is a vicious and cruel sport. The main premise behind cockfighting is that you take a rooster, take away his freedom and teach him to hate his fellow creatures. You make him angry, and instill in him a desire to fight to the death, all at the same time making money in the process. That's why I won't get involved in the sport," replied Preach.

"There's more important things in this world than money, like helping save the human race."

"You know that in order to get Al ready to fight, were going to have to do a lot of work. Right now, he's just a battle stag not a battle cock," said Teach

"What be a 'battle stag?'" asked Amos.

"That's a rooster that's less than two years old. Capone has to be conditioned, you know, trained, maybe we can have him spar with another rooster?"

"Al Capone still be having his natural spurs on his legs," replied Amos, "one of these days we gonna have to remove the spurs and put on knives."

"You mean those sharp blades that they put on the gamecock's legs?" asked Preach, "how inhumane, how inhumane."

"They gots to be put on the rooster's legs, or in he can't be fighting," replied Amos.

"For sparing, you can use sparring muffs," said Teach, "a cover they use over the spurs. Eventually we're also going to have to trim off his comb and wattle with a razor blade."

"You do what you need to do," replied Preach, "It sounds cruel and inhumane just the same, and I just don't want to be a part of it."

"You know we're running out of cash again," said Teach, "It just seems like we're always having to figure out how to come up with more money. I'm sick and tired of wading through traffic, trying to come up with ways to convince people of giving us a hand out."

"You know that El Cabron guy?" asked Amos, "He made us an offer, but I bet the boy's willing to give us a lot more."

"If you sell little Al to that man, you'll be giving the poor bird a death sentence," responded Preach.

"You're right," said Teach, "at least if we own him, we can stop a fight before he's been killed by the other bird."

"If we get a chance," countered Preach.

"But if El Cabron is the owner," continued Teach, "if Capone merely loses and is still alive, he'll finish off the bird to teach him a lesson."

As they came closer to their home under the bridge, the three were approached by Ebenezer. "Your buddy, the guy they call El Cabron, came by," he told the three, "He says to tell you that his offer to buy Al Capone is now 'three thousand dollars,' but if you refuse, he's 'not gonna buy the bird at any price.'"

"The next match is this coming Friday, so you've got less than a week to think about it, that's what he said for me to tell you."

Chapter Twenty-eight:
Research

Next morning the three headed off to breakfast in a somber mood. "Why so sad?" asked Debra as they sat down to eat at the Christian House of Charity. "It's Flathead," answered Preach, "they're really trying to put the screws down on him."

"You be meaning what they really want to do is Screw Him," responded Amos

"I don't understand," said Debra, "it seems as though they don't really care about the truth, nothing seems to make sense."

"Today I'm heading off to the library to see what I can find out," spoke Teach, "they have Wi-Fi there, but I don't have a computer."

"That's no problem at all," spoke Debra, "I have one that I can loan you. It isn't the most upgraded as I just got a new one, but it's great for online research."

"That would be fantastic," replied Teach, as he leaned over and their eyes met, lips almost touching, "I don't know how I'm going to be able to thank you."

"Maybe let's get together for another dinner sometime soon," said Debra, "Tomorrow Night?" "Sounds great," replied Teach, as their lips touched.

"Oh, I can't stand this mushy stuff," said Amos, as he puckered his lips and made kissing sounds in the air."

"I can deal with the mushy stuff," replied Preach, "so long as something good comes out of it for Flathead."

"Listen you guys, I'm going to have to head off to the library, do you want to come with me?" "Sounds like an excellent plan." answered Preach, "we need to do whatever we can, as fast as we can."

"I'll be helping too," replied Amos, "I be good at research." "The more the merrier," replied Teach, "I'll be giving both of you assignments."

"Look at him," Preach, referring to Teach, "It's as if he's rediscovered his calling, the one that was long lost, as if he's back in his teacher of the year mode."

All three headed off toward the main library.

As they sat down at a table, Teach took a small paper notebook out of his pocket. "Here are your assignments," he looked at Preach and Amos.

"Preach," I want you to find out all that you can about "Right to Counsel."

"Amos," I want you to find what you can about being tried twice for the same crime, I think they call it 'Double Jeopardy.'"

"Me, I'm going to research the charges. After we're finished, we'll try and make sense out of all this."

Amos and Preach scattered in different directions, as Teach set up his laptop computer and began hurriedly hitting the keyboard with his fingers.

"Let's start with 'Continuing Criminal Enterprise,'" Teach spoke to himself, as he typed, "okay here it is."

"Let's, see, it appears that five or more people must be charged, that's why there are five people listed in the indictment."

His next words, almost loud enough for others in the library to hear were "Holy shit!"

"In Order To Find A Defendant Guilty Of Engaging In A Continuing Criminal Enterprise, The Government Does Not Have To Prove That All Five Or More People Operated Together At The Same Time, Or That The Defendant Knew All Of Them."

The Cockfight

"What kind of shit is this! What kind of shit is this!" "Shush!" came a response from a few people around him in the library as they looked at him with slight annoyance.

"Now," let me see what this '851' thing is. He began read what came up on the screen and saw something about "Notice of intent to seek enhanced penalties." He was directed to another federal statute, "18 United States Code Section 3559(c)."

This one was titled, "Mandatory Life Imprisonment," he expelled a whistling sound from his mouth as he read. "Mandatory Life Imprisonment," "Notwithstanding any other provision of law, if a person has one or more serious drug offenses."

"Wait a second," he spoke to himself, "Flathead is going to jail for life, for his two drug felonies. And they wouldn't even have been felonies if he had had the money to pay for his court appointed counsel?"

Then Teach saw something that made him really angry, he read that in some states a person is allowed to grow as much marijuana as he wanted so long as a doctor verified that it was a "medical necessity." "This is just like Flathead, who needed the marijuana, after he suffered a bullet wound to the shoulder while saving his buddies," he thought to himself.

But how is it that the Federal Government is able to punish the defendant for a crime that he already paid for in state court? With that, Amos and Preach came back to show Teach what they had found.

"Well," said Amos, "This be what we be finding, but first, let me be apologizing cause I ain't too bright. My last grade of formal education be the sixth grade, so excuse me ifn I don't talk too well." "You'll do fine," replied Preach, "Just tell us what you know."

"Seems like we had a revolution against this King George the 3rd of England, it also seems like he had a bad and corrupt justice system, where people never received fair trials, or something called 'Due Process of Law.'"

"In order to protect the people from the same abuses, we enacted something called the Bill of Rights. Am I doing okay?" asked Amos. "You're doing

A+," said Teach, "Keep talking."

"Lookie here at this Fifth Amendment, it be sayin that 'no person be subject for the same offense be twice put in jeopardy of life or limb. Then it also says that they not be deprived of that thing called 'Due process of law.'"

"What I ain't be figuring out yet," said Amos, "is how these folks be getting around it all?"

"Let me show you something else I found," said Preach, "they call it the 'Sixth Amendment,' and this one says that an accused 'Shall Have Assistance of Counsel.'"

"I haven't figured out yet how they're getting around this one either, but I'll come back and tell you after we've done some more research."

The three went back to work.

Chapter Twenty-nine:

Continuing Criminal Enterprise

"Okay," said Preach after a couple of hours, Amos at his side, "I think we've got our answers but I don't think you're going to like them."

"I ain't be liken any of this," said Amos, "but here how they be getting aroun all the laws and trashin people's rights."

Preach continued, "It seems that the reason we had a rule against double jeopardy was because of what at one time had been happening in Merry Old England. What happened was King Henry VII didn't like the fact that juries were giving what he felt was lenient treatment for criminals, so he was allowing them to be tried again in different counties. This did not sit right with the people."

"By the time of our independence, the idea that a person should not be subjected more than once to punishment for the same acts had become widely accepted.

"But we had a problem here, the problem was that a Federal Government was now being substituted for a King. You see," said Preach, "People like Thomas Jefferson and James Madison, who wrote the bill of rights, demanded protection from this new monarch, that monarch being the federal government."

"They didn't want the federal government stepping in after a state government had found someone not guilty of a crime. The federal government gets around this by saying things like "We're a different sovereign and this is a different crime.""

"But be catchin this," said Amos, "The acts all be the same."

Preach continued, "They use that excuse and say that their interpretation of 'double jeopardy' is that you can't be tried in the state courts twice for the same thing or the federal courts twice for the same thing."

"I ain't very smart," Amos continued, "but why would there be a Bill of Rights if it wasn't for protection against this new federal government? Why would they say that the double jeopardy thing would apply separately for a state prosecution and then separately for a government prosecution, that wouldn't be making no sense at all?"

"Now's where it really gets rare," replied Preach, "they say they're separate sovereigns, but when they go to punish you, they punish you twice, first for violating the federal law, then for prior convictions in state court. For those prior convictions, they're apparently not a 'separate sovereign.'"

All three started chuckling.

"Let me tell you what I've found out about the Right to Counsel and the money Flathead had to pay to his court appointed lawyers," said Teach. "It turns out that the federal courts up there had been doing the same thing, but they were doing it after the conviction and sentencing.

"A federal appeals court found that that was wrong, still they collected millions of dollars from people whom they had no right to collect the money from, and apparently they've kept that money."

"But the State of North Carolina continues doing it. Only, they won't even let a defendant take a plea until he pays up. They've taken millions of dollars from people who don't owe them a thing."

"What's more," continued Teach, "is that they're calling crimes 'felonies' where these are misdemeanors or infractions everywhere else. In other places

The Cockfight

the subject penalty is less than a year in jail, and sometimes just a small fine, like a traffic ticket."

"By convicting them and calling it a felony, they take away a defendant's civil liberties, including their right to vote. They're pulling this bullshit all over the South. In Alabama, there are more blacks in jail than in college."

"Black man live his life as a slave to the system," added Amos, "and in the end he dies."

"They've also come up with these things called "Sentencing Guidelines," continued Teach, "they were supposed to make sentencing fairer and more uniform, but instead they put everyone in jail and throw away the key. In 1971 when they were first enacted, there were 330,000 people in jail in this country.

"Today, there are 490,000 prison guards, watching a prison population of 2.3 million people. It costs $50,000 a year to incarcerate one inmate, and that's more than it costs to pay a teacher like me. There are five times as many people per capita in prison than in Great Britain. Are the people in America five times as evil, or is the system five times as evil?"

"So let me be getting this straight," replied Amos, "They be taken money from people they ain't supposed to, and they be callin the crimes they commit something that they ain't. They be taken away their right to vote, and they be sending them to these local jails so that the jails can make money while they be in there. They be sentencing them to life in prison for what ain't even a felony, and what even be legal in some states, and they be callin it a 'Justice system?'"

"Like I say," I ain't too bright," Amos continued, "but ain't it similar to what you said Flathead be charged with, a 'Continuing Criminal Enterprise?'" "But not a 'Continuing Criminal Enterprise' run by the criminals, a 'Continuing Criminal Enterprise,' run by the ones in charge?"

"It would almost be funny if it wasn't true," replied Preach, "It would almost be funny."

"I think it's time to leave," said Teach, "It's been a long day." The three men left the library and slowly headed back to the bridge.

"I don't know what we're going to say to Flathead," said Teach, "there's really no good news in any of this."

"We're going to have to do some praying," replied Preach, "but not just for Flathead." "What do you mean?" asked Teach.

"We're going to have to be praying for this entire God Forsaken country. We've forgotten our roots, we've forgotten why we fought so hard for our independence. We've gone back on our word and our promise to the people. Those in charge are more interested in lining their own pockets than in any form of justice, it's a sad thing, a sad thing."

"But there's still one thing I do know," continued Preach. "What's that?" responded Teach. "Without prayer, we haven't got a prayer."

Chapter Thirty:
Tomorrow Night

The next morning rolled around with anticipation as Teach, Preach and Amos headed off for breakfast. "Thank you for letting me use your laptop," Teach spoke to Debra, "We've found out a lot."

"Is any of it good?" Debra asked. "Not really, answered Teach, "but at least we know what he's up against."

"Satan, Satan, is what he's up against," Preach chimed in, "but I know who's stronger," and he looked upwards.

"We can't see Flathead until visiting day," continued Teach, "and that isn't until tomorrow evening."

"That's good," Debra whispered in his ear, "that means we can spend the evening together. Let's say we meet over at the Cuban American Cafe for dinner at seven?"

"Sounds like a plan," Teach responded.

"Whooeee," said Amos as they sat down at their table, "Looks like tonight, Teach gonna be given private lessons."

"Oh lay off," responded Teach, "It's just a date."

"I'm not a genius," said Preach, "but I think you had better get a hold of some clean clothes, wash up a bit, and look respectable for the lady. Amos and

I can head back to the bridge and feed Al Capone."

"What I'll do," responded Teach, "is buy a new shirt." "There's a laundromat over on Northwest 36th Street, it's a long walk, but at least I'll be able wear clean clothing. They've got a bathroom there too, so I'll also have a place to get washed up."

"You'd better get a haircut as well," added Preach, "I don't mean to tell you this, but you're looking kind of ragged."

"Can you help me with some money?" Teach asked Preach and Amos. "Here's a twenty," answered Preach." "And here's another," said Amos.

"You guys are the best friends anyone could have," replied Teach

"It ain't be about friendship," responded Amos, "I be lookin at it as an investment. One day you gonna be back on top, and when that day happen, we gonna need some help too!"

They headed off in different directions, Preach and Amos for the bridge, and Teach for the long walk to the laundromat.

Upon entry, he took off the backpack he was wearing, one that was holding his spare clothing, along with the computer that Debra had given him. As he dumped his clothing into the washing machine, the computer almost went in with it.

"Better not wash this," he thought to himself, "as he put the computer on a table behind him."

Before he could say "Jiminy Cricket," a teenage kid grabbed the computer and took off running.

"Son of a bitch," said Teach as he ran off after the kid, but it was too late, as the thief disappeared around a corner with his take.

"I don't know what I'm going to tell Debra," Teach said to himself out loud, "I hope she won't miss it."

After spending an inordinate amount of time in the bathroom at the rear of the Laundromat, washing himself from top to bottom and getting dressed in clean clothing, several people knocked on the door. "Hey, what's going on in there?"

"Hold you horses," answered Teach, "I'll be out soon."

Teach exited the bathroom and headed off for a haircut.

"Hey mister," said the barber, "Nice weather we're having." "Sure is," replied Teach, "sure is."

"Say, how long has it been since you had a haircut?" asked the barber, "You definitely look ready."

"Oh, sometimes I just let it go," answered Teach, "sometimes I just let it go." The barber snickered.

"Fresh, clean shaven, and wearing clean clothing, Teach started back on the long walk to Seaside and dinner.

"I've never seen you look this good," said Debra, "and you smell nice." "Well," replied Teach, "fine duds for a fine lady."

Debra came closer as they both looked into each other's eyes. "You know, my apartment is just a few miles away, why don't we head over there for a drink after dinner?"

"Sounds great," answered Teach, "I'd love to."

Meal over, they drove off in Debra's small compact car. "Nice car," said Teach, "It's been a while since I've been driven around, most the time I just walk from place to place."

"It's not a great car," replied Debra, "but it's what I can afford on what the state pays me."

"You know," said Teach, "you have the most beautiful eyes of any woman I've ever met."

"Oh," you're just saying that, "she responded."

"No, I mean it, they're as blue as the Atlantic Ocean."

"You know you're not so bad yourself," she responded, as she fumbled for the keys to open her apartment door.

As the door opened, they both fell on the floor, tearing at each other's clothing. "Let's go to the bedroom?" she said, and both of them hurriedly disrobed and embraced each other on the bed. It was several hours before the two finally fell asleep, later awoken by an alarm clock.

Debra turned off the clock and the two kissed. "Boy, were you special," said Debra, "how long has it been?" "It's not that it's been a long time, it's just that I've never been with a woman like you."

"I've got to work today," she sighed, "so I'll make some breakfast, then head off to the shelter."

"It wouldn't look right if they saw you taking me there," said Teach, "so I'll just walk home."

"Why don't you let me take you home," replied Debra, "I'd like to see where it is that you live."

"No, it's a mess, and besides it's not fit for a lady like you."

She looked disappointed.

Both of them kissed and went on their way.

Chapter Thirty-one:
No-One Here by That Name

"So, what your date be like?" asked Amos, "you be lookin real happy."

"Oh," replied Teach, "it was okay."

"I'll bet it was more than okay," Amos responded, "a lot more."

"Listen," said Preach, "today is visiting day, and we've got to see Flathead. No matter what, we've got to keep his spirits up."

"We really don't have any good news to tell him," replied Teach, "Maybe we shouldn't tell him anything at all."

"Perhaps you can do some more research, on that computer?" asked Preach.

"Oh, the computer," answered Teach, "some little bastard grabbed it when I was at the laundromat. He took off and I couldn't catch him."

"Did you tell Debra?" asked Preach

"No, we were too busy doing other things."

As the day rolled on, Preach reminded Teach and Amos that it was time to start heading out toward the Dade County Jail.

"We had better start moving along," said Preach, "let's grab dinner at Saint Maria's. The wheelchair led train headed off for Saint Maria's. It was when they arrived that they were surprised to see Debra.

"I thought I'd find you here," she said, "I wanted to tell you that I'm concerned about Flathead. I went to see him earlier today and they wouldn't let me in. I asked, and no-one would tell me anything about him."

"This doesn't bode well," replied Preach, "this doesn't bode well."

"I'm concerned as well," Debra sighed.

"Look," said Teach, "maybe us three can go and see what they tell us."

"And I have some bad news," Teach said to Debra, "Someone stole the computer you lent me."

"Oh, don't worry," replied Debra, "It was my spare." "I hope you didn't have anything important on it, did it?" asked Teach.

"Nothing important, just client records, addresses and social security numbers, nothing important," she shook her head, but in mid shake showed a concerned look.

"That be good," said Amos, "that be good."

The three headed off to the jail.

"We have no-one here by that name," replied the guard at the front window.

"Can you be checkin that again?" asked Amos. "No sir, no-one by that name."

"Well," said Teach, "they've probably sent him back to North Carolina." "I hope that's the case," replied Preach, "I hope that's the case."

After the attempted visit, they headed back for the bridge for sleep.

Next morning as the three entered the Christian House of Charity, they could see Debra with her head in her hands. She was looking down at a newspaper and appeared to be crying.

"What's wrong?" asked Teach, "what's wrong?"

She pushed the paper toward him and ran away, still crying. The headlines read,

"MAN FOUND HANGING IN JAIL CELL." Teach began to read the article out loud.

"A man was found hanging yesterday from a bed sheet in his cell at the Dade County Jail. William Smith was pronounced dead by the Medical

Examiner at three p.m. Mr. Smith, a native of North Carolina, was being held pending an extradition hearing which was going to occur today.

"An ex-military man, he was facing felony drug and assault charges. Mr. Smith appeared to be in 'good spirits' according to the staff at the jail," Teach looked at Preach and Amos as he read, "So everyone was surprised at the turn of events. His body will be shipped back to North Carolina where he will be buried with full military honors."

"Full military honors? Full military honors?" lamented Preach, "the bastards never stood behind him when he was alive, and now they think they can assuage their dirty consciences by giving him 'honors' now that he's dead."

"Here's another article, it's an editorial about the 'high suicide rate' in the military. "Here's what it says," Teach read,

"Suicide rates in the military are at record levels. The rates are not likely to get lower. One of the reasons is the lack of mental health treatment for soldiers who come home from service. We ask a lot of these soldiers, so it's important that we give them their due when they return. 'I'm not sure what the problem is, except that they have trouble adjusting to the outside world upon their return,' I quote a Major General who recently stated this in an article, 'These boys deserve better.'"

"These boys do deserve better, signed, An American."

"If the military had stood behind him, he would never have had the issues he had," responded Teach, "And if the country had stood behind him, he would be recognized for the true hero he was. But these bastards don't give a shit, their only interest in America is how much money they can line their pockets with."

"What a shame, what a shame," said Preach, "When we get back, I'm going to send his belongings including his medals, back to the military. Then I'm going to write them a letter, a good letter. One that really tells them who this boy was and what they did to him, one that tells the truth."

Chapter Thirty-two:

The Letter

"Can I see what you be writing, Preach," asked Amos. "Why don't you just read it out loud?"

"I'm not quite finished," answered Preach, "give me a few more minutes."

"I've packed up his backpack and the medals," Teach responded, "we can send it back, care of the United States Army."

"Sound's good," said Preach, "Does anyone want to listen to what I wrote?"

Teach, Amos, Ebenezer and several others gathered around.

"Dear United States Military Man, or should I call you 'Uncle Sam'? Enclosed please find the final possessions of a man who gave everything he had for your army, but got nothing in return. Enclosed you will find a Silver Star for heroism and a Purple Heart as well. If the United States had exhibited a tenth as much heroism toward this boy as he gave to you folks, he would still be alive today."

"When he suffered pain from a bullet wound to the shoulder, you just turned your head. When he got caught up in an unholy and ungodly justice system, you just pretended that he didn't exist. Yes, he gave his all for the army, and in return you are giving him a burial with full military honors. I'm sure that as a dead man he really appreciates that. But I kind of feel that you should have given the effort to stand by him when he was alive, When He Was Alive. . ."

"Sincerely, A Man Who Knows A Little Bit About How God Works."

"That's a good letter, Preach," said Ebenezer, "short and to the point. But do you think anyone's going to read it?" "We'll see, we'll see." Everyone sat there moping glumly.

"Remember that tomorrow is Friday," Ebenezer looked at Teach, "that El Cabron guy is going to ask if you've taken his offer."

"Three thousand dollars or three million dollars, Al Capone is not for sale," answered Teach, "not at any price." "That be right," added Amos, "that be right."

"You see," said Teach, "some folks have morals that aren't for sale." "Not at no price no how," Amos finished the thought.

As tomorrow evening approached and it started getting darker, people with their 'tackle boxes' started arriving under the bridge. They commenced setting up the lights and the cockpit was made ready. A scale to weigh the roosters was put in place and the man with the hat started calling out for bets.

"So, what be the big match tonight?" asked Amos, "I be hopin to make some money tonight."

"It's El Cabron's bird again, it's undefeated and we're looking for a challenger."

"El Cabron thought that you guys might be interested in fighting that Flarry Eyed Grey you have against his bird."

"Ain't be no way Capone be fightin tonight, sides he's still got a little while to go forin he's ready."

"Hola Seniors," said El Cabron loudly as he approached Teach and Amos, "have you considered my offer? Three thousand big ones."

"Yes, we've considered your offer," replied Teach, "and he's not for sale."

"Then why don't you let him fight my bird, if he's such a fine bird he should be able to whip Rojo in a minute, maybe two."

"Look," said Teach, "we're not fighting him till he's ready, and he's not for

The Cockfight

sale, not at any price." "You got that right," said Amos, "You got that right."

Pretty soon the ticket taker announced the first match, a brown bird versus a bantam rooster. "You be bettin on this one?" Amos asked Teach. "No, said Teach, you know I always wait for the last round, besides I don't have any money." "Tells you what," said Amos, "Here be a hundred dollars. I be bettin it on the bantam. If he wins, I split it with you." "You don't have to do that," replied Teach. "No, it just be payin you back for some of the money you done give to me."

The two dubbed roosters, their wattle and comb removed, were put beak to beak in the pit. The bell rang and they went at it, legs kicking feathers flying. Before long the brown rooster was bleeding profusely from the neck and back. Within a minute more he was down, breathing his last.

"We be winning we be winning!" screamed Amos, "counting his money and giving half to Teach." "Three hundred dollars apiece, that's not bad," replied Teach. "Well, it ain't chickenfeed," responded Amos.

"Why don't you check on Al?" asked Teach, "I just have a queasy feeling." "Okay," said Amos, "I be right back."

As Amos got close to Capone's cage, he saw a couple of men sitting in front of it. One of the men was reaching behind his back and trying to unlatch the door.

"Amos rolled his heavy wheelchair right on the man's arm." "Cojones!," screamed the man, "what the fuck are you doing." "I tell you what the fuck I'm doing," responded Amos, "I be stopping two chicken thieves from making off with my rooster." "Hey, we weren't doing anything," said the other man. "The hell you weren't," replied Teach, as a crowd now gathered.

El Cabron now stepped forward. "Get out of here you chicken thieves, you aren't welcome here anymore." With those words, the men ran off.

"I chased them away," said El Cabron, "they won't be back." He put his hand on the handle of a gun that stuck out of his pants.

"Come on, let's get on with the matches, on with the matches!" screamed the bet taker, and everyone scrambled back to the cockpit."

"Listen," said Teach to Amos, "I'm going to stay here for the rest of the night, you can go watch the matches. We've got a valuable gamecock and someone has got to guard him."

When the matches ended, Amos came back. "So, how'd you do?" asked Teach. "Well, I thought I be doing okay until the last match, then I saw that Rojo Alabama be fightin this yellow legged hatch. The odds be favorin Rojo twenty to one, so I figured on a big payday and bet on the hatch. Boy I be wrong, lost everything I had."

"Well, here's half of what I have," replied Teach, "it came from you anyway." "Yeah," responded Amos, "but you a standup guy, a standup guy."

Chapter Thirty-three:
The Philosophy of Vagrancy

> "I ain't got no home, I'm just rambling round,
> I'm just a rambling worker I roam from town to town
> The police make it hard wherever I may go
> And I ain't got no home in this world anymore."

There are many reasons for homelessness in America today, but those words, written by the immortal Woody Guthrie still ring true. Many people choose the homeless life because they are nonconformists. They like the idea of living in an unstructured society where other people can't tell them what to do. They live by the well-worn adage of, "Nothing to do and plenty of time to do it."

They like the idea of living in the great outdoors where there's no time schedule, the idea of living in the fresh air and waking up to blue skies. It is a pure and unadulterated philosophy unencumbered by complicated concepts such as "responsibility" and thoughts such as "Maybe I better do this or do that."

Ebenezer was such a person. He chose to live under the bridge because he wasn't going to live in a society "where everyone out there are 'liars and hypocrites.'" He was a true man of the world and that world he lived in embraced him, that world being his friends who also lived with him under the bridge.

When Ebenezer started puking up dark red blood coupled with thick green mucous and other viscous matter, there was concern amongst the other bridge residents.

"Hey man, you be all right?" asked Amos, as Ebenezer coughed and choked, spitting out red laced phlegm along with what appeared to be pieces of lung.

"I'm okay," he replied as he choked, "just a little under the weather."

"That don't sound too good, maybe you ought to head out to the hospital."

"Yeah," said One Lip pointing to his disfigured face, "they took care of my problem, and treated me really well."

Everyone glanced at One Lip, and the mouth that looked as though it had been partially gnawed away by some half-crazed demon.

"Look," said Teach, "if you aren't better in a day or so, we're going to wrap you up in a blanket, tie you down and carry you to the doctor."

"I'll be okay, I'll be okay," he sputtered as he choked.

"When we hit breakfast, I'm going to run this by Debra."

At the Christian House of Charity, Debra was concerned. "I've heard that there's a tuberculosis scare going round," she said, "you had better get him straight to the hospital."

When they returned, things hadn't gotten any better. Ebenezer was lying down, breathing heavily. His face had taken an ashen pale color.

"Okay Amos, out of your chair," ordered Teach, as Preach and Teach both lifted him out and to the ground, "we're going to have to borrow it to wheel Ebenezer over to The Dade Memorial Public Hospital."

They placed Ebenezer in the chair, put a blanket around him, and commenced the two-mile trip to the emergency room.

"You going to be doing just fine," said Preach, "the Lord's gonna look after you." No response came from Ebenezer as bloody drool leaked from his mouth.

When they finally reached the emergency room, there was a crowd of people in line.

Teach walked up to the nurse receptionist at the window and asked "How long will it be?" "We've got a busy day today," she responded, "there's seven people ahead of you being treated for gunshot wounds. Take these papers and fill them out."

"What are these papers?" asked Teach. "Just things like medical history, insurance, you know, all the questions that have to be answered before the hospital can treat him."

"We don't know anything about his medical history and I don't think he's got insurance," said Teach.

"Then it's going to take a little longer," replied the nurse, "back in line, please."

They had arrived at the hospital at 9:00 a.m., but when 7:00 p.m. rolled around they were starting to lose their patience.

"Can't you see the man is dying!" screamed Preach, "Don't you have any humanity? Aren't you a hospital???" "Listen sir," replied the nurse, "we're operating on public funding, I'm sorry if things are not happening as quickly as you want but we do the best we can."

A doctor in scrubs walked by, "What seems to be the problem?" he asked, as he glanced at Ebenezer, blood and phlegm now staining his blanket.

"Oh my God," said the doctor, "that man's sick!" "You think so?" replied Preach. With that, the doctor screamed at the nurse, "get the orderlies and get this man into quarantine, stat!"

"I guess our day is at an end," said Preach, "time to head on back. "Yeah," replied Teach, "I hope he's in good hands, I just hope he's in good hands." "We'll have to pray about that one," Preach responded, "Just pray."

CHAPTER THIRTY-FOUR:

I'd Rather Be Fishing

One of the great things about South Florida is sunny weather and the availability of many outdoor sporting activities.

One of the most popular activities is that of fishing. Living under a bridge, next to a bay, provides access to waters which are pretty well stocked with all sorts of sea creatures.

Fishing is a great sport, and doesn't really take a large investment. You don't need a boat, only a large handheld spool of fishing line, a hook and some bait. Bait comes in all forms and sometimes an unlikely form of bait can result in surprising things.

"What's that you be fishing with, One Lip?" asked Amos.

"Lettuce, lettuce I saved from a tuna fish sandwich I got at the All Day And All Night Convenience Store," was the reply.

"What you thinkin you gonna catch with lettuce?"

"If the tuna fish liked it, some other fish might too."

Suddenly One Lip screamed "I Got ONE!" Residents of the bridge came running down to look, "And He's A WHOPPER!"

As everyone crowded by, it became a tug of war. One Lip would pull the creature four or five feet toward him, and the creature would pull One Lip back four or five feet.

Back and forth, back and forth.

"I don't know what you got," said Amos, "but it be fightin like an angry bull."

"Not so much like a bull," responded Teach as he looked at the creature from the edge of the rocks, "More like a cow. You've hooked a sea cow!"

"A goddamn sea-cow!" came the response.

"Yeah," replied Teach, "they call them manatees and they're protected, so you better not let anyone see what you've hooked."

"Should I cut the line, should I cut the line?" asked One Lip. "No, don't do that," replied Preach, "that would only allow the animal to suffer."

"Then what should I do? what should I do?" "Well," answered Teach, "that's a complicated question, but I remember teaching a history class once where we read about the early Florida Indians. I think they called them 'Caloosahatchee' or something like that. They say that they used to cook and eat manatee regularly, that it was a local delicacy."

"Maybe that be why they be callin it 'sea-cow,' like steak," responded Amos, "Maybe I be liken some filet mignon of sea-cow?"

Teach spied a Marine patrol boat heading towards them from the south.

"How you boy's doing?" said a man from the boat. "Just enjoying a nice day of fishing," replied One Lip, as they waved and the boat went on its way.

Just then, one of the bridge dwellers pointed at the animal. "Look, he's rolled over dead."

"Poor boy," said Preach, "must have died from the shock."

"Look," said the scruffy looking man with dark features, "I used to be a chef at La Figaros, and I can cook anything."

"We've got to figure out a way to get it out of the water," said Teach, and with those words another man produced a rope. They looped it around the dead sea-cow's neck and proceeded to drag it onto shore.

"Quick," said the man, "hold up a blanket so no-one sees what I'm doing." Next, he produced a knife and went to work.

"Okay, look," he said, "I've got sixteen good cuts of steak from this manatee, er sea-cow. We need a barbecue pit, charcoal, starter fluid, matches and seasoning."

"We can be heading off to the grocery store and pick up all them things," replied Amos, "Come on Teach, Preach, let's have a barbecue."

The wheelchair led train headed toward downtown, then north on Biscayne Boulevard toward Proberty's Superfood Store.

"What you be thinking be a good seasoning for filet mignon de sea-cow?" asked Amos. "I don't know," responded Teach, "but stop me before I ask anyone."

"The poor creature," added Preach, "If he had known that he was going to end up as the main course meal for some homeless people, I'm sure he'd have thought twice about eating that lettuce."

"You know," said Teach, "I'm going to turn this into a history lesson, how would the Caloosahatchee have cooked sea-cow?"

"I be bettin they had lemons, seein this is Florida," replied Amos. "Good idea," replied Teach, "let's get a dozen lemons." "I would hazard a guess that they also had watermelon," added Preach, "seeing that this is the South, they probably had it for dessert." "That be soundin really good," said Amos.

"An I be bettin they had these here crinkled potato chips, seein as potatoes grow from the groun up. An I be awfully sure they had a few sixpacks of Mickies best lager beer."

"No, I don't think so," replied Preach, "Indians didn't drink alcohol."

"Ifn you say so," said a slightly disappointed Amos.

Excitement flooded the entire bridge community upon their return. Soon the smoke of a barbecue could be seen and the smell of barbecued manatee wafted through the air.

"It's the patrol boat!" as the boat could be seen returning from the north side of the inlet. "What did you do with the bones?" Teach asked the man now known as 'Chef.'"

"We buried them," he responded, pointing to an area of sand where a few ribs could be seen sticking out of the sand.

"So how are you boys doing?" asked the smartly dressed marine patrol officer, "we saw some smoke and just wanted to check it out."

"Oh, we just be havin a barbecue," replied Amos, "you be wantin some?"

"That sure does smell good," responded the officer, and the Chef cut off a small piece of manatee steak, speared it with a plastic fork and gave it to him.

"Boy, this is the best steak I've ever had, interesting flavor, interesting flavor, you boy's just keep on having a good time." The officer headed back toward the patrol boat.

"And they say the homeless life is a hard life," the officer said to another officer as he got back onboard, "these boys have it better than we do, eating steak!"

Chapter Thirty-Five:
Let's Get the Hell Out of Here

Next morning at the Christian House of Charity, Debra approached Teach with a proposition.

"Look," she said, "I've got a long weekend, let's get the hell out of here."

"Where do you want to go?" asked Teach

"I don't know," she answered, "why don't we go to Orlando, lose ourselves in the insanity?"

"We could hit a theme park or two," replied Teach, "it's been a while but they're always a lot of fun." "That sounds great," said Debra, "and don't worry about the money, this one's on me."

"Where and when do you want to meet?" she asked. "Why don't you pick me up in front of Seaside at 7 p.m., I'll be packed and ready to go."

"Fantastic," she responded, "we'll have a great time," and she kissed Teach on the lips.

"Looks like I'm gonna be gone for the weekend," Teach told Preach and Amos, "you guys make sure that Al Capone is okay."

"Oh, we will," replied Preach, "you just have a good time, we'll take care of him."

Seven o'clock rolled around and Teach was packed and ready. "You smell good," said Debra, as he sat down in the passenger seat.

"Best cologne that Burdocks sells," he replied, not mentioning the fact that he was the beneficiary of a free sample.

As they traveled on, the pleasant conversation made the hours go by quickly.

"So, were you really teacher of the year?" asked Debra. "You can look it up," answered Teach, "they still have my plaque on the wall at the school board, the bastards."

"Well, I guess that that's something that they can never take away from you. What about your wife and kids, do you ever think about them?"

"Well, I do think about the kids, the witch never stood by me. As soon as the newspaper articles came out, they convinced her that I was some kind of monster. She ended up with the house, the retirement, everything that I owned."

"Too bad," she responded, "life is so sad, so sad." "Yeah," said Teach, "but I'll never let it defeat me. The best thing that ever happened to me was when I met Preach and Amos. They taught me to keep looking up no matter what happens, they taught me that the most important thing in life is 'attitude.' You're only defeated when you feel like a loser, when you let them change your attitude."

They started looking for a hotel. "Here's one that's not too expensive," said Debra. "I just hope the bed's good," replied Teach, and they embraced each other in the car.

"What name are you signing in under?" asked the man at the reservation desk. "Mr and Mrs. Debra, oh, Mr. and Mrs Bradford. . ." The clerk snickered.

"Here is my license," said Debra, "we're checking in under my name."

As the two approached the hotel door, they embraced again. Falling into the bed, they spent the entire evening and most of the morning making love.

The Cockfight

"Where do you recommend that we go?" Teach asked the desk clerk next morning, "Do you have any discount tickets?"

"Oh yes," answered the clerk, "Here are tickets to the new Horatio Potato Exhibit at Quidmar Studios"

"I loved that entire series," said Debra, "I read every last one." "Yeah," replied Teach, "I used to read those stories to my kids, brings back memories."

They headed off to Quidmar Studios and the Horatio Potato theme park.

"Look" said Debra, "It's Horatio Potato himself!" A man in a potato outfit, dancing and laughing, approached, "Hi! I'm Horatio Potato!" said the man, as he danced around, kids screaming, "I'm from the land of Au Gratin!" "Isn't this great," said Debra, "Lets head to Cheeseland!"

The two held hands, lovers in love with the fantasy they found themselves in and in love with each other.

"You know," said Teach, "I haven't had this much fun, since, since . . , and a tear slowly ran down his cheek.

"Don't worry," replied Debra, "one day the nightmare will end, I promise you that one day it will end." They embraced and passionately kissed.

That evening they found themselves in a restaurant. "You know," said Teach, "you're the best thing that's happened to me in, in I don't even think that I can remember." "And you're the best thing that's happened to me," replied Debra, "why don't we head back to the hotel."

"So did you have a good time today?" asked the desk clerk as the two tightly held hands. "The best, the best," answered Debra," as Teach and Debra's eyes met and they embraced in another passionate kiss.

The desk clerk shook his head and chuckled.

Next morning, they packed the car and headed back toward home. "Listen," said Debra, "I'm not sure where it is that you live, but I want to offer something that I've thought about," she continued, "I want you to think about moving into my apartment."

"That's a wonderful offer you're making," he replied, "but there are things that I'm still fighting in my mind, baggage left over from those fake and contrived charges that they foisted against me. I don't want my problems to become your problems, and for now, I think it's best that we keep things separate."

"I know you've been through a lot," said Debra disappointedly, as they pulled up to Seaside, "but I want you to know that I believe in you." The two of them again embraced, and as she drove off, they captured each other's gaze.

Chapter Thirty-Six:
Thirty Days to Fitness

"Lookie here" said Amos, pointing to an ad in an old tattered magazine, "this ad be saying that anyone can be like that Charles Atlas guy in thirty days, 'Anyone.' That mean even a rooster."

"I don't know about that," replied Teach, "but we're definitely going to have to get this rooster in fighting shape."

"Lookie here again," said Amos, "I done tied this red ribbon on a stick, watch what happens when I put it in front of the bird."

He stuck the stick with the red ribbon through the cage bars and brought it back and forth past Al Capone's face, repeating this procedure over and over again. The bird paid little attention, and appeared more interested in its cup filled with food.

"Say," Amos said to the rooster, "how you gonna get in fightin shape if you're more interested in eatin than fightin?"

"Maybe the bird's not into fighting," replied Preach, "maybe this bird has a higher calling." "What kind of calling that be?" asked Amos. "I can't say for now," answered Preach, "only time will tell."

"I've got another idea," said Amos, "I've heard that if you put a mirror in a rooster's cage, that he gonna think that it's another rooster and it make him angry. What he do is he fight his reflection in the mirror."

"I think that Ebenezer had a mirror with his stuff," replied Teach, "why don't we give it a try and put it in the cage?"

You could hear One Lip as he went rummaging through Ebenezer's belongings. "Here it is," he responded, coming back with a five or six-inch hand held grooming mirror.

"Well," said Teach, carefully opening the door and placing the mirror in the corner of the coop, "let's see how he responds."

On the far side of the cage, Al continued pecking at a corn-cobb that had been placed there near his food bowl. Soon, however, his curiosity was piqued. He glanced at the mirror several times and then commenced picking pieces of food out of his feathers and from under his wings.

"I be damned," said Amos, "the boy's groomin himself." Then, upon finishing the procedure, the bird strutted directly in front of the mirror. He leaned one way, then another, observing his reflection with keen interest. He stood tall, then squat. Then he turned to one side, continuously looking at his image.

"Now he be admiring himself, he be seeing which side is his best." "I don't know about this rooster," replied Teach, "but something tells me that he's more show rooster than gamecock."

"I'm telling you," said Preach, "that he's got a higher calling"

"Why don't we take him out for some exercise?" asked Teach. "That would be a grand idea," answered Preach, and they looped the string around Al Capone's neck and tied it to Amo's wheelchair.

"Where should we head off to?" asked Teach.

"I don't know," answered Preach, "why don't we take a walk in the Peacock Park?" The wheelchair led train headed back across the bridge toward the mainland and north on Biscayne Boulevard.

"Peacock Park is a good place to stretch out one's legs," said Preach, "a good place to just relax."

The four headed off on their way, Amos, pushed by Teach, Preach, and a Flarry Eyed Grey rooster named Al Capone.

As they approached the park, they could see children on swings, young adults playing volleyball, and families having barbecues.

"Well, I tell you," said Preach, "isn't it nice to see families having fun, people just happy being alive, enjoying the day and the sun." Teach became melancholy, thinking about his own life and a past world he once lived in and treasured.

"You know," replied Teach, "we never really treasure the things we have until they're gone." "That be true, that be true," said Amos, "you know I never did think much about my legs, they was just something that got me aroun from place to place. But now that they don't work, I thinks about em a lot, a lot."

"We have many blessings that we don't count," responded Preach, "we should count every-one, every-one." They could hear the sound of children screaming with delight and laughter as they tossed a ball to one another.

As they walked along a little further up a path near the bay, Al in tow, a sound emanated from under one of the bushes. It started as a barely audible but serious "meow," then a "hiss."

"What that be?" asked Amos, as he glanced around.

CHAPTER THIRTY-SEVEN:

CAT SCRATCH FEVER

The large yellow tomcat approached the rooster in a crouched position, hissing and snarling as he sprang at the bird.

"Out of here! Out of here!" screamed Teach, as the cat pounced on the rooster. Soon all that could be heard was loud screaming and squawking as the cat and the bird both rolled and fought with each other across the ground.

"Let him loose! Let him loose," yelled Preach, "he can't fight all tied up," and with a struggle, Amos broke the string that tied the bird to the wheelchair.

Both the tomcat and the rooster fled in different directions.

"Did you see where he went? Did you see where he went?" asked Teach. "I think he flew over to those bushes over there," pointing toward a row of dense foliage.

The three came over to the area, calling and calling for the Flarry Eyed Grey. "Here Al, Here Al Capone," "Here chicky chicky," "Here chicky chicky."

As hour after hour passed, they looked in every nook and cranny of the park. "I hope we haven't lost him," said Teach, "I hope we haven't lost him." "He be a great bird," Amos lamented, "he be my best friend, my best friend."

"Listen," replied Preach, "if God wants him to come back, he'll come back. But we musn't get discouraged, God always puts us where he wants us to be, and only where he wants us be."

"It's getting late," said Teach, "we had better head back, we can resume the search tomorrow."

As the now three members of the sad wheelchair led train headed back to the bridge, "Amos looked back toward the park in despair." In a second, though, his attitude changed. "Hey," he declared, "look who be following us home."

"Well, I'll be tarred and feathered," replied Preach, "if it ain't our feathered friend."

Preach walked over to the rooster. "How you doing, little fellow?" The rooster gave a little cackle. You look like you've lost a few feathers, but otherwise you gave that rotten cat a lesson he probably won't forget. Would you like a lift home?" and with those words the Flarry Eyed Grey hopped up on Preaches shoulder, and home they went.

"You know," said Amos, "I bet that cat never seen a whuppin like he done got from Al Capone. "I'll bet you're right," said Teach, "did you see the way that the cat ran when you untied him, he ran like a bat out of hell."

"It's been a long day," replied Preach, "When we get back, I'm going to get some shut eye."

The next morning, they headed out to breakfast. Upon arrival at the Christian House of Charity Debra looked glum. "Why so down?" asked Teach. With that She pushed a newspaper toward him with an article that read, "Department of Social Services Investigated For Release of Personal Information."

The article went on:

"The Department of Social Services is being investigated for a leak of confidential and private information. Several individuals have been victimized through the theft of information such as addresses and social security numbers.

"Fraudulent credit card applications as well as fake tax returns have allegedly been filed in these individual's names. According to a spokesman for the FBI, "we have an ongoing investigation, but as for now, it appears that the information came from a state-owned computer. We cannot comment until the investigation is over with."

"Well," said Teach, "it wasn't your fault." "No, but I'm worried that they're going to blame someone," she replied. "Well, I wouldn't worry, at least they're going to catch that person who stole your computer."

As the three sat down for breakfast, Apache and No Brains approached. "We heard that Ebenezer was in the hospital, have you heard anything about him?"

"No, but when we're done eating, we'll heading out to the hospital to see how he's doing," replied Teach. "Yeah, we be real concerned about the boy, real concerned," chimed Amos.

"I don't know if we should expect good news," said Preach as they made their way toward Dade Memorial Hospital, "we best do some praying."

Soon they found themselves at the hospital reception room.

"Excuse me," said Amos to the receptionist, "we be here to inquire about our friend Ebenezer, the one we be bringin to the hospital last week."

"I remember," said the receptionist, "he's still in quarantine, other than that we have no new information."

"When do you think that the boy might be released?" asked Preach. "Sorry, but I have no further information," was the only response.

"I hope the boy gonna be okay," replied Amos as they walked away, "I just hope that the boy gonna be okay."

"Listen," I'm concerned about Debra as well," said Teach, "she looked pretty down about that article concerning the names and address of her clients that they stole," he pulled the article out of his pocket.

"Oh, I wouldn't be worryin about that," Amos responded, "it weren't her fault that the computer be stolen, and sides she had nothing to do with it."

A little further down was a partially torn story with a headline that read,

"FBI CONTINUES INVESTIGATION INTO KENTUCKY CRIME LAB"

Teach shoved the article back into his right pants pocket.

Chapter Thirty-eight:

A Stranger

"Rollie sure do ask a lot of questions," said Amos, "That boy done wanna know everything that's going on."

"You mean that guy that showed up a week ago?" Teach responded, "I'm kind of leery about that one, he seems to want to be our friend. He keeps on asking all sorts of questions, and when you ask him about himself, he always gives different answers."

With that, a skinny white guy in his mid-twenties, with a tattered t-shirt, grubby pants, and dirty hair arrived from somewhere on top of the causeway.

"Hey, guys," said the man. "Hello Rollie," replied Teach.

"Hey look man," replied Rollie," you guys know where I can get some weed?" Rollie produced a joint from out of his pocket and lit it up."

"Listen," said Preach, "we're not the ones you should ask. But why don't you take your whacky tobbacky and smoke it somewhere else."

"I'm sorry," said the man, "I just figured that you might know where I can find some Acapulco gold."

"We're a Christian organization replied Preach, "we're into none of that." While Preach spoke, several bridge dwellers, dressed in tattered clothing and dirty shirts, looked on."

"Yeah," said Amos, "we be the Twelve Apostles and Preach here be our leader."

"That's right," chimed Teach, "see the holes in our clothing, its holy clothing." They all laughed.

After that, Rollie departed. "You know what's strange about that guy?" Teach pointed out, "he shows up around the same time every day, and leaves about the same time as well, it's as if he's on some kind of schedule."

"Yeah," I be noticing that too, and he be asking a lot of question about Al Capone." "What did you tell him?" asked Teach.

"I be tellin him that Al be our egg-layin bird." "But he's a rooster," responded Teach. "Yeah," replied Amos, "but I kind of feel that the light in that boy's head isn't bright enough to know the difference."

"So, tell me about that article you've been reading, Teach," asked Preach, "the one about that FBI crime lab in Kentucky."

"Well, it says here in the article that 'One technician failed to follow proper procedure when analyzing DNA samples.' This happened in at least 'one hundred and three cases' and she's been indicted for giving false testimony." "Here's what she says; 'I have to admit that it was worse than being evasive or not correcting the record, it was simply not telling the truth.'"

"Holy Mother Mary," replied Preach, "maybe this has some connection to your case?" "You know," replied Teach, "maybe it could. But I don't have the money to hire a lawyer or do the things that are necessary to try and find out if my case was one of the ones where they lied."

"You know your lady friend might be a good person to talk to," responded Preach, "she seems to have a good heart."

"Maybe you're right," answered Teach, "I'll talk to Debra tomorrow morning."

"Has anyone heard anything about Ebenezer," sputtered One Lip, concerned about his long-time friend.

"Last we heard," said Preach, "is he's in some kind of 'quarantine,' they won't tell us anything else."

Chapter Thirty-nine:
Descended from Monkeys

The next morning, Preach, Teach and Amos headed out on their wheelchair led train to the Christian House of Charity.

"You know," said Preach, "I don't believe in this evolution stuff. God created Adam and Eve, and put them on this earth six thousand years ago, I just don't buy the proposition that we're descended from monkeys."

"You know," replied Teach, "I didn't believe that either. That was until I had the misfortune to meet some of the individuals involved in my arrest, in my mind there's no doubt that they were definitely related to some lower species."

The three exited the serving line and sat down with their breakfast. "Hey, lookie here," said Amos, "today we got pancakes, and the scrambled eggs not be mixed with the bean curd. This gonna be a good day, a good day!" he smiled.

"I sure hope so," replied Teach, and he waved to Debra.

"What is it, you seem excited?" asked Debra as she sat next to Teach. "We'll I don't know if I'm excited or not," Teach said, and he pulled the article out of his pocket.

"I'll read it out loud."

"SEVERAL INDICTED IN FBI CRIME LAB SCAM"

"Several individuals working for the FBI crime lab in Louisville Kentucky have been indicted for giving false testimony in cases involving identification through DNA analysis. At least one individual has acknowledged that she gave false testimony in no less than one hundred and three cases. She says that she 'admits that it was wrong and that it was worse than being evasive or not correcting the truth, that she was simply not telling the truth.'"

"This is horrible," said Debra, "but what does this have to do with you?" "Well," replied Teach, "I was convicted using DNA evidence. I was forced to take a plea because they said that there was a match between my DNA and the DNA they took from the victim, that student of mine."

"You mean?" and Debra grabbed his arm. "Yes," responded Teach, "I'm certain that this was the same crime lab that did the analysis in my case."

"What can we do? Who can we speak to?" asked Debra. "Well, that's the thing," answered Teach, "somehow we're going to have to get a lawyer to look at my case, but I don't have any money, heck, I don't even have a home."

"Look," said Debra, "whatever it takes, we'll find you a lawyer. If I have to sell everything that I have, I'll figure out how to pay for it. I'm going to help you . . . I'm going to do everything I can to help you," she held his arm tightly as tear streamed down her face.

"Look," said Preach, "we can try and raise money as well."

"Where are you going to be able to raise money for a lawyer?" responded Teach. "Through the kindness of strangers," responded Preach, "through the kindness of strangers."

"Yeah," said Amos, "and through our patented fundraisin system," and he pulled the three signs from beneath his wheelchair, the ones that read "Will Work For Food," "Will Pray For Your Soul," and "Wounded In Action."

"You're an angel," Teach said to Debra, "and you guys are the best friends that anyone could ever have."

"We'd better leave them two alone," Preach glanced at Amos, "they look like they need to talk privately." Preach and Amos departed for another table.

"Listen," said Teach to Debra, "I don't know how to thank you."

"Don't thank me yet, first, I'm going to have to find an attorney who's willing to look at your case. I'm going to have to ask around."

"Look," said Teach, "whatever you can do is fine with me, already, you've given me hope. And that's something I haven't had in years."

Both kissed, tears streaming down their faces.

As Amos and Preach began to leave, Amos asked Preach, "Do you think this Debra lady can help Teach?" "I have no doubt," replied Preach, "I have no doubt," and he looked up to the heavens.

Pretty soon, Teach caught up. "Well," said Preach, "you're looking chipper."

"I don't know if it's going to lead to something, but I know this, I know that attorneys are expensive and we're going to have to get to work raising money."

Soon they found themselves back under the bridge.

"What about Al Capone?" asked One Lip, "You could sell him to El Cabron and that would help raise the money."

"No," replied Teach, "He isn't for sale, not at any price."

Chapter Forty:

Bad News

One week later, the three were approached by Debra as soon as they arrived for breakfast.

"Well, I tried as best as I could to find an experienced attorney but fees ranged from $10,000 to $50,000, and that was just the down-payment," she lamented, "I was however able to find an attorney who does work for the poor. He doesn't have much experience in complicated federal criminal matters, but he's willing to do whatever he can to help us."

"How long has he been practicing?" asked Teach. "My understanding is that he passed the bar exam a year ago, but he's very enthusiastic."

"Has he ever handled any criminal defense matters?" "He told me that he once successfully defended a man 'charged with speeding.'" "You've got to be kidding," replied Teach, 'speeding?'" "Yes," answered Debra, "but it was a serious charge, ten miles over the limit."

"Ten miles over the limit," laughed Amos, "In Miami that be called obstructin traffic." "What do you think, Preach?" asked Teach as he turned away from Debra.

"Sometimes miracles happen in the most unexpected of ways. If God delivered the pitiful Jews from mighty Egyptians, he can accomplish this miracle as well.

"Okay," said Teach, "when can I meet with him?"

"I've made an appointment for 1 p.m. this afternoon," replied Debra, "You had better head back and clean up. I'll pick you up at Seaside."

A few hours later, Debra pulled to the curb and opened the door of her small compact car. They headed north, up Biscayne Boulevard to North Miami Beach. A half hour later, they found themselves in a sparsely decorated waiting room where a receptionist busily juggled phone calls and put out what appeared to be serious brush fires.

"Yes, Ms. Winslow, Mr. Hooper has been working on your problem and he just doesn't have an answer yet. Yes, Ms. Winslow, I know all about your rude neighbor and how he lounges by his pool, naked as a jaybird, and in clear sight from your bedroom window. Also, how he speeds down the street in his car and shoots you the finger, I just don't have any information on the status of the restraining order."

She clicked the hold button. "Hi, can I help you?"

"Yes," responded Debra, "We're here to see Mr. Hooper."

"Have a seat, it will be a little while."

After approximately one hour, they were welcomed into a small office where a young smiling attorney sat behind a desk.

"Hi, I'm Robert Hooper and you must be Mr. Bradford," said the man as he introduced himself. "I am," Teach replied, "I hope you can help me."

"Well, I'm glad you asked that question. This is a very interesting case, and I like interesting cases."

"How so?" responded Teach.

"Well, we have a situation where the government is already aware that there are problems relating to DNA identification and its use in previous cases. I went and reviewed your file and found that yours was one of the cases that the Kentucky crime lab handled."

Debra clasped Teaches arm.

"But we've got to overcome one sticky issue." "What's that?" asked Teach.

"The fact that you plead guilty to the charge."

"But I had to," responded Teach, as he lowered his head into his hands, "they told my lawyer and he told me that if I lost at trial they would seek 'life in prison,' that they had never lost a DNA identification case, and according to my lawyer, this was a 'crapshoot.'"

"How much do you charge?" Teach asked, as he looked at Debra. "Don't worry about that, I'm taking care of it," Debra responded, "Mr. Hooper has an idea."

"I do, here's how I'm going to handle it. I'm going to start with a letter to the Assistant United States Attorney who handled the prosecution for the government. I'm going to put our position down on paper and request that he move to re-open the matter. If this man has a heart and a soul, he'll see that there was a problem with your case and he'll agree to review it."

Chapter Forty-one:
The Letter For Reconsideration

To: Office Of United States Attorney
Care Of: Assistant United States Attorney Jack Ratley
Southern District of The State of Florida

"Dear Mr. Ratley,
"This letter is to advise you that I have been retained by Richard Bradford to represent him with regards to newly discovered evidence in relation to his criminal conviction for Interstate Transportation of A Female For Immoral Purposes.

"This conviction was based upon a plea entered by the defendant to the charges. Specifically, as you may recall, you were the prosecuting attorney in the matter of United States versus Bradford. In the discovery provided to the defendant, it was put forth that the DNA of the defendant had been obtained from the victim.

"A lab report was prepared by the F.B.I. crime lab in Kentucky. Based upon a determination by this lab, and the low likelihood that the DNA retrieved came from any party but the defendant, (less than one in a billion), and further, based upon the threat of "life in prison" upon conviction, Mr. Bradford entered a guilty plea. Prior to entry of this plea, he had steadfastly maintained his innocence.

"Now it appears that the individuals at the Kentucky crime lab perpetrated a fraud on the court. This fraud involved perjured testimony, false and contrived results, and failure to properly test subject samples.

"Individuals working for this lab have admitted to outright fabrication of results and lies, in no less than one hundred and three cases.

"This is to request that you agree to a joint motion requesting that the court re-open this matter with the goal being that the court order new tests be conducted by an independent crime lab."

"Your response to this letter is eagerly anticipated."

Sincerely Yours,
Robert Hooper Esq.

The Response:

"Dear Mr. Hooper,
"I have received and reviewed your letter. As your letter accurately reflects, your client plead guilty to the charges. Independent evidence, in the form of eyewitness testimony, also points toward the guilt of your client in this matter.

"I am aware of the issue with the crime lab, but unfortunately cannot agree to a request that the court re-examine this matter or order additional testing and analysis of DNA results."

Respectfully,
Jack Ratley

"Why won't he agree?" asked Debra, "clasping Teach's arm, "isn't he interested in the truth?" "You know," responded attorney Hooper from behind his desk, "that's a good question. The American Bar Association has rules relating to what a prosecuting attorney's role should be. I'll read it to you, it says,"

"When a prosecutor knows of new, credible and material evidence creating a reasonable likelihood that a convicted defendant did not commit an offense which the defendant was convicted, the prosecutor shall promptly disclose that evidence to the defendant, unless a court authorizes delay."

"But he told me nothing," Teach responded, "I had to read about it in the newspaper."

"I'll read on," said Hooper, as he read from the rule book, 'The prosecutor must undertake further investigation or make reasonable efforts to cause an investigation, to determine whether the defendant was convicted of an offense the defendant did not commit. When a prosecutor knows of clear and convincing evidence establishing that a defendant in the prosecutor's jurisdiction was convicted of an offense that he did not commit, the prosecution shall seek to remedy the conviction.'"

"You see," said Hooper, "the role of a prosecutor is not merely to convict, but to seek justice."

"But it's like they don't care," said Debra, "as if they just don't give a damn."

"Where do we go from here?" asked Teach.

"I don't care what it costs," replied Debra, "Somehow, some way, we'll find the money."

"Well," responded Hooper, "there's a way to attempt to attack the conviction in civil court and reopen the case. It's called a 'habeas action,' and it's complicated, time-consuming, and expensive."

Chapter Forty-two:
A Day In The Sun

"The reason I've called this meeting," said Preach to the fifty or more vagrants, transients and homeless men gathered around him, "is because one of our good friends needs our help."

"Teach needs to raise money to pay for a lawyer to help him prove that the government's charges, for which he served ten years in prison, are bogus."

"He is not guilty of anything, but in this land of the free and the brave, there is something that is far from free, that thing being justice."

"How much does he need?" asked one scraggly man with missing teeth.

"It's a lot of money," responded Preach, "He's going to need ten thousand dollars just to get started."

No Brains stepped forward. "I'm willing to donate half of my whiskey budget right here and now, all for my good friend Teach." Preach put his arm around him, "Now there's a man after God's own heart."

"I be having a plan," said Amos, "but it gonna be needin everyone here," and with that, he pulled several signs from under his wheelchair. "We be needing to make signs for everybody, we be needin to hit the street and raise money for our good friend."

"Let's be lookin like professional bums, we'll hit the convenience store and buy a marker and use some scrap boxes to make more signs. We got to do this in a coordinated way."

"That's a great idea," responded Preach, "let's get to work. But there's one last thing," he added, "We can't let Teach know what we're doing."

The fifty scraggly men, otherwise known as bums, vagrants, hobos, homeless men, miscreants and deviants set off on a mission, the first part of that mission being to make signs.

Hard at work, signs reading "WILL WORK FOR FOOD," "STARVING VET," "NEED HELP FOR MEDICAL ISSUES," "HOMELESS AND HARMLESS," "ONCE I OWNED A RAILROAD," and many others slowly came into being.

"You be spellin homeless wrong," said Amos, looking at a sign in which the "e" was missing. I done learned that from Teach!"

"Better yet, maybe he should leave it like that," answered One Lip, "looks more authentic."

"Yeah," responded Amos, "We ain't just ordinary bums, we be 'authentic' bums!"

"Alright everybody," said Preach in a loud voice, "let's hit the streets."

And with those words, fifty hard scrabbled men exited from under the General MacArthur Causeway, high spirit visible in every man's eyes.

Aggressive in both their determination and their mission, they approached every car at every intersection at every red light in downtown Miami.

Particularly effective were No Brains and One Lip. One Lip would lie down by the side of the road, drool dripping from his mouth. No Brains would approach a car and knock loudly on driver side windows. "Help me, help me, I need money to get my friend to the doctor!"

Invariably, windows would open, people would throw coins, dollar bills, spare change, anything they had, out of the window. Then, as soon as the light changed to green, they'd hop on the gas and speed off.

When evening rolled around, everyone watched as Preach counted the money. "We've had a good day. Not quite there, but five thousand dollars isn't too shabby."

"I've got a good tip on next week's cockfight," replied No Brains, "Dr. Sevrin's got a new rooster, a Shanghai, and he wants to get back at El Cabron. I'm told that this is the meanest fighting rooster God ever put on this earth."

"So, what are you saying?" asked Preach

"I think we could raise the rest of the money by putting it all on the Shanghai."

Chapter Forty-three:
The Shanghai Rooster

"Oh, do you remember sweet Betsy from Pike, who crossed the wide mountains with her lover Ike? Two yoke of oxen a large yeller dog, a tall Shanghai rooster and one spotted hog."

"Preach has been whistling this song for two days now, what's going on?" asked Teach.

"It has to do with nothin we be discussin," replied Amos, "as they sat under the bridge, a breeze blowing cooling down what otherwise would be a typical steamy hot Miami day.

"You guys are up to something," responded Teach, "Everybody under the bridge gets quiet when they see me, like they know something that I don't know."

"Tis a wonderful day," responded Preach, "just a fine day for whistling," and he continued on, whistling the same tune he'd been whistling for the last three days.

"Should we tell him?" asked Amos. "Well, he's going to find out anyway," answered Preach.

"We and the boys be out raisin money for your lawyer fees," replied Amos. "You what?" responded Teach.

"That be right," Amos continued, "we all went out on the street and collected five thousand dollars."

"Five thousand dollars, you've got to be kidding me!" "He's not kidding you," replied Preach, "all the boys hit the street, begging and panhandling as if their lives depended on it."

"I don't know how I'm ever going to repay you, no-one has ever done anything like this for me before. You guys are the greatest in the world," said Teach, tears streaming down his face.

"You don't have to repay anyone," answered Preach, "We did it because we care about you and we want you to fight the bastards that destroyed your life."

"There be more to it than that," responded Amos, "No Brains here be havin an idea." "That's right," replied No Brains, "Dr. Severin's got a new bird, a Shanghai, and he's supposed to be the meanest bird anyone ever saw."

"So, what are you saying?" asked Teach. "Well," answered No Brains, "the Shanghai is going to fight El Cabron's rooster."

"It's a two for one shot, and if we bet against El Cabron and win, we can raise the ten thousand dollars."

"But you could also lose five thousand," replied Teach, "and that would be hard to replace." "I'm not a betting man," said Preach, "but something tells me that this time you might get lucky, somehow, God is in the mix."

"Debra says that she is going to pay the attorney the money to get started, but I know she doesn't have it. Since this money isn't really mine, I can't tell you guys what to do with it. But if it turns out that we win the bet, I'll do whatever I can to repay it, whatever I can."

With that, Al Capone, in his nearby cage, burst out with a happy cackling noise.

Chapter Forty-four:
Fight Night

"That's a fine bird you've got there," said El Cabron, "sitting in front of Al Capone's cage. "I've heard you say that before," replied Teach.

"Yes, and I've heard that you need to raise some money," responded El Cabron, "and in the interest of helping you, I've decided to raise my offer to five thousand dollars."

Amos looked at Teach, "You be knowin that that be all you needing to get that attorney started on your case." "I know," replied Teach, and then he turned around and spoke directly to El Cabron.

"Al Capone is not for sale, not for any price!"

El Cabron walked away, a disappointed look in his eyes.

Soon, more and more people gathered under the bridge as the evening's festivities got underway. "Taking bets, taking bets," yelled the man with the hat. The cockpit was made ready and lights were set up. As a scale to weigh the fighting roosters was assembled, crowds of bettors gathered around the cages, in order to assess each fighting bird's chance at victory.

"There's a huge crowd today," said Preach, "bigger than usual." "You're hanging around?" responded Teach, "you usually take off before the fights begin."

"This time," replied Preach, "something's telling me to stick around, it's as if something important is going to happen."

The bell clanged and the first bloody fight of the night began. Two bantam roosters went at it, kicking, fighting, slicing and dicing each other until the floor of the pit was blood red.

Finally, after two minutes, one gave way and lay on the ground dying, gasping its last breath. Cheers went up from the crowd, as well as a few sighs. With every bet there are winners as well as losers.

Hour after hour went by, as the matches became more interesting to the bettors. Almost three hundred people now crowded under the bridge. Until, finally, it was time for the grand finale, the big match.

"And now, the final match," screamed the announcer. "Place your bets now." No-Brains approached the ticket taker, "Five thousand dollars on the Shanghai."

"That's a pretty big bet, I hope you win," said the man as he took the money. "So do I," replied No Brains, "So do I."

A large crowd gathered around the cockpit as the two cocks, placed nose to nose, were released, released to fight, gouge, kick and tear each other to pieces. At the clang of the bell, they went at each other as if hell, fury and damnation had all been released at one time.

Screaming and yelling ensued as the ball of feathers, legs with sharp knives attached, became indiscernible amidst the horrendous ferocity of the combatants.

Blood came from somewhere, but no-one was sure from where? "One of them's been sliced!" screamed No Brains, "but I'm not sure which?"

All of a sudden, a loud gasp was let out by the crowd as the Alabama fell to the dirt, furtively flailing its legs. As the poor bird lay dying, El Cabron began to curse.

"Goddamn Bird, you lousy piece of shit, you're as worthless as any bird I ever saw," he entered the pit and kicked the dying bird with all his might.

A crowd gathered around Teach as the money collected from the win was handed over to him. This time, tears were in everyone's eyes.

Chapter Forty-five:
The Long Row To Hoe

"Okay," said the lawyer to Teach and Debra, "I'm going to read a part of what I am filing with the court. It's entitled "Motion To Vacate Sentence Under 28 United States Code Section 2255."

"Defendant Richard Bradford, through counsel, moves the court to vacate the sentence handed down in this case on the grounds that the conviction for Interstate Transportation Of A Female For Immoral Purposes was obtained in violation of the United States Constitution and the laws of the United States; thus, Mr. Bradford is currently serving a sentence based upon said invalid conviction. This motion is based upon the United States Constitution, the Memorandum of law in Support of the motion is attached."

"But he's not serving a sentence," replied Debra, "he's already out of jail."

"I'm glad you brought that up," replied the lawyer, "under the law, in order to be accorded relief, a defendant must either be in prison or jail, or else have his or her liberty under some form of restraint as part of a federal sentence."

"But he's not under what you call federal restraint, is he?" she asked. "I'm afraid he is, when they handed down his sentence, they also gave him five years of what's called 'Supervised release,' that's not up for another six months. I'm also worried about another thing."

"What's that?" asked Teach. "Have you been in touch with your Supervised Release Officer?"

"No, I'm afraid I haven't. He used to visit me when I lived under the Julia Tuttle Causeway with the violent sex offenders, but after things got rough, Preach and I left for better digs under a different bridge. I haven't seen him since."

"Well, here's the issue, once you file this document, you're back on the radar screen. If they want to, they can file papers alleging the fact that you have violated your conditions of supervised release by moving to a different location and not communicating with them."

"Let me get this straight," said Debra, "In order for Richard to show that he's innocent, he risks admitting that he violated terms of his sentence that never would have been handed out in the first place had the government crime lab not lied, and he never would have been convicted of anything?"

"That's about the size of it," answered the lawyer.

"If you're ever going to clear your name, you've got to stand up to these liars," spoke Debra to Teach, "you've got to show them that they can't ruin people's lives on lies and falsehoods. You've got to take a stand for what is right,"

"Go ahead with it, Mr. Hooper," Debra tightly clasped Teach's arm, "There's a time in a person's life when one must stand up to injustice and now is my time."

"Thank you for the payment," went the lawyer, "this is enough to get things started. I'll try and keep my fees low, but depending upon the position that the government takes in this matter, it could become costly."

"We'll figure it out," replied Teach, "we'll figure it out."

"It could be a long row to hoe," replied the attorney, "There will be hearings, at least one. We've got to convince the judge that an injustice occurred. The government is going to fight to the bitter end, they know that what they did was wrong, but they'll never admit to it.

"The problem is that they supposedly stand for "truth and justice," but the reality of the situation is that those within the system will ignore those principles to protect their own careers."

"So, tell me again how you raised the money?" asked Debra as they were leaving the lawyer's office, "Is it really true that Amos, Preach, One Lip, No Brains and all the other guys went out and hit the streets begging and panhandling to raise money for you, their friend?"

"It's really true," answered Teach, "it's really true." "That must have been quite a sight," Debra laughed, "listen, why don't you reconsider my invitation to move in with me in my little apartment? It would be just the two of us and we could be together and I could help you with your case?"

Chapter Forty-six:
Notice of Hearing

As Teach, Amos and Preach waited in line at the Christian House of Charity, they knew something was up when Debra ran over to Teach. "You've got a hearing!" said Debra, "and it's only three weeks away!"

"Well," replied Preach, "the Lord's been working hard and fast in your direction."

"I spoke to the lawyer and he subpoenaed both the girl who accused you as well as the lab technician who lied."

"I'm a little nervous," said Teach, "It's been nearly thirteen years since I saw that girl." "You mean the one with the cigarettes who lied about you and her?" asked Debra, "I'll bet she's quite a sight."

"As diseased as her soul is," maybe the Lord will reach out and touch her," replied Preach, "She sounds like a good candidate for the Lord's love."

"What about the lab technician," asked Amos, "she be a candidate for the Lord's love too?" "That's a tough one," responded Preach, "but maybe she needs it more than anyone."

As they sat down and ate their breakfast, Teach looked toward Amos and Preach and thanked them again for helping raise the attorney fees. "You know," said Teach, "the lawyer says that it could get to be expensive, 'depending upon how hard the government fights.'"

"We be with you," responded Amos, "no matter how hard the government be fightin, we be fightin with you."

"As they walked out of House of Charity to the street and the bright South Florida day, Preach looked at Teach and his now tattered looking clothing. "We've got to get you looking good before the hearing, we'll put some money together to get you a wash and shave, maybe a new suit from the Goodwill."

"Yeah," responded Amos, "you can't be looking skunky in front of no judge."

"You know," said Teach, "I've been thinking a lot about Al,"

"Me too," said Preach, "Me be three," said Amos.

"You know, we can't let him fall into the hands of El Cabron, if he gets a hold of Capone, he'll kill the bird as soon as he loses his first fight."

"Yes, this is true," said Preach, "but what about the money you could get by selling him? It would help your case."

"Ifn worse come to worse, me and the boys can go out collectin for you," chimed Amos, "Our patented collection system be workin real well."

"Let me think about it a little while," replied Teach, "let me think about it."

"So, are you going to get together with Debra?" asked Preach, "you know you two would make a fine couple. It's been a while since I performed a marriage ceremony, so I might be a little rusty but no-one has ever complained about the job I did."

"Now you're pushing him," said Amos, "his face is red all over."

"Listen," you guys, "I'm not going to do anything until the time is right. I've got a lot of things to resolve in my life, and I don't want to throw my problems on anyone else."

"Sometimes a good woman is exactly what you need," observed Preach, "you should think about it."

The three headed on toward the thrift store. As they entered the door,

Amos asked the cashier, "Where be your finest men's suits, for my friend who be pushin this chair?" "Over there," was the response, "We're having a two for one sale today."

"That be great," replied Amos, "my green suit be showin some wear, and a new purple one be just the thing the doctor ordered."

"I think you'd better look for a more conservative suit," Preach warned Teach, "a purple suit in court would be looked upon as some kind of heresy."

As they looked through the racks, Teach found a grey suit. "This one appears to be my size," he said to the others, "I'm going to go and try it on."

As he emerged from the dressing room, the two stared at him in amazement. "You be lookin like a different man," said Amos, "a different man."

"Lookie here what I found," and Amos held up a purple suit, pants, and a white straw hat, "this be my two for one."

Chapter Forty-seven:
Back from The Dead

When he first appeared under the bridge, it was like an apparition, something with a ghostly appearance.

"He be back, he be back!" screamed Amos, "Ebenezer be back from the dead!"

Everyone under the bridge ran over to see their long-lost friend.

"So, how's it been?" asked Preach with a booming voice, "you look like you've been through the ringer!"

"I'm okay," replied Ebenezer, his voice tired and his face pasty white from months in the decontamination ward." "I'll tell you all about it," he said, "but first I've got to sit down." No Brains and One Lip grabbed his arms and helped him as he sat on a large rock.

"They finally let me go, but they had to have permission from the Center For Disease Control in Atlanta." "Atlanta!" spoke Preach with a loud voice, "Why Atlanta?"

"Well, they said that I had some kind of what they called a 'pernicious disease,' that they hadn't quite seen anything like it before and they wanted to make sure that I was okay before they let me go."

"They used all these experimental drugs on me and at one time I had four doctors regularly checking me out. They flew in some specialist from Johns Hopkins in Baltimore Maryland to look at me. I think he wrote some kind of research paper, got his PhD. on a discussion of whatever it is that I caught while living under the bridge. They named it 'MacArthur Causeway Fever.'" "You can look it up."

"Well, if that don't beat all," replied Preach, "What do you think about it, Teach?" "Well, said Teach, "it might just be another reason for all of us to get the hell out of here. Living under a bridge has never done anyone any good."

"What's eating him?" asked Ebenezer, "He's the first person I wanted to see when I returned."

"A lot has happened," answered Preach, "Teach here has a hearing coming up in court. He's found an attorney who's going to fight the false charges that sent him away and destroyed his life."

"Well, if that don't beat all," replied Ebenezer, "That's wonderful news."

"He also has an invitation from his girlfriend." "You mean that Debra lady from the Christian House of Charity?" "That's right," said Preach, "She wants him to move in with her."

"So why don't you do it?" asked Ebenezer, "Would you rather be living under a bridge?"

"I think he be worried about the commitment," replied Amos, "and he be remembering what his first wife done do to him."

"Ah," said No Brains, "she was a someone who never really cared about you. You've got to know the difference between a woman like that and an angel standing by you."

"You know, you're right," answered Teach, "Whoever started calling you '"No Brains'" was far off the mark, you are one of the smartest people I know," and he walked over and put his arm around him. "I've just got to think about it a little longer."

"I think that what be eatin him is he don't have no money for a ring," Amos whispered to the others, "but we can take care of that, that ain't no big deal."

"No, that ain't no big deal," said No Brains, "I got at least six gold teeth that the guy at the Seebild Building was interested in, said he could melt them down and make a ring for me."

"Let's sneak off, you, me and Preach, and see that guy at the Seebild."

Amos, pushed by No Brains, went off on their way. "Where you going?" asked Teach, "Where are you going without me?"

"We're just going out for a little sunshine," answered Amos, "a little Miami sun."

"But I'm the one who's supposed to be pushing you," said Teach, "Why is No Brains taking my place?"

"Now lookie here," replied Amos, "you ain't the only one who can push me around, they be these other guys as well."

All three went off on their mission.

"Open Wide," said the man at the third-floor shop at the Seebild Jewelry Center in Downtown Miami, as he looked inside of No Brain's mouth with a pair of glasses, magnifiers attached, "those are nice specimens."

"Do you think you can be makin an engagement ring out them?" asked Amos. "Yes, I think I can," and he produced a large pair of pliers.

"I'm going to need some help," answered the jeweler, "someone to hold him down while I pull these fillings out."

Amos pushed his wheelchair up against No Brains, forcing him against a counter, while Preach held No Brain's mouth open.

"There, there," said the jeweler as he clamped the pliers on a tooth in the rear of No Brain's mouth and began to yank. With one vicious pull, the tooth came out. "Now that was easy, only five more to go."

"You know," said Amos as he, Preach and No Brains, in obvious pain and holding a bloody rag on his mouth, walked back to the bridge, "this be only for the engagement ring. We gonna have to raise some more money for the wedding ring."

Chapter Forty-eight:
The Big Day Coming

"Well tomorrow's the big day," said Preach, "maybe we ought to say a little prayer." Preach, Teach, Amos, One Lip, No Brains, and Ebenezer gathered in a circle.

"Dear God, please extend your grace to this poor school teacher who was punished for only doing his job. May you protect him from the evil one who would seek to destroy him, and may you do this for your own glory." Everyone surrounding joined in an "Amen." Al, in his cage, let out a "cluck" as well.

"I don't know what to expect," said Teach, "but I feel a lot better." "Just remember that we'll all be in the courtroom with you, we'll be backing you up," replied Preach.

"I know, and I can't thank you guys enough."

"Are you gonna be seein Debra fore the big event?" asked Amos. "Yes, we're going to have dinner tonight at Seaside.

"Me and the boys be gotten something for you, well, not really for you." No Brains produced a small package and handed it over to Teach.

"Now what is this, what could you guys have gotten, and what do you mean 'not for me?'" "Why don't you open it up and see," responded Amos.

He opened up the package and found a ring with a small diamond, "It be a present for you to give to Debra, an engagement ring."

"Now wait a second, you guys can't make me . . . you guys . . . I need to think about this."

Teach walked off to a corner of the concrete abutment and sat down and descended deep into thought.

"Okay," said Amos, "It's been ten minutes already, what you be deciding?"

Teach returned, "Look, I'm carrying around a lot of baggage, it's unfair to put it all on someone else. What if she says 'no?'"

"I don't think either of those issues are going to be a problem," replied Preach, "You've just got to decide if this is what's in your heart."

When seven p.m. arrived, Debra and Teach met outside of the door of the Cuban American Café. "Let's get a seat in the back where we can talk," said Teach.

"Tomorrow is the big day," replied Debra, "how do you feel?"

"Well, I feel a little nervous," said Teach, "It's been so long since things happened, that I would have a chance of clearing my name, of living a normal life, of, of, of falling in love."

He got down on one knee. "Debra, will you marry me?" "Yes! Yes!" was the response as they kissed and embraced. Others looking on at the café' began clapping. He placed the ring, a ring made of gold that formerly resided in No Brain's mouth, on her middle finger.

"No matter what happens tomorrow, no matter how the court rules or how the cards fall, I'm the happiest man in the world," said Teach. "Me too!" responded Debra, and they embraced again.

"Go pick up your things and spend the night with me at my apartment," said Debra, "That way you can get cleaned up for the morning before the hearing. I'm taking the day off and will sit as close to you as I can. Let me drive you back to get your belongings."

"Well, you might as well see where I live, but it's not the Hilton." "Listen," she said, "I've been in every sorry place in this decrepit city, I've seen people who lived in boxes and in alleyways, I've seen houses crawling with

The Cockfight

rats and roaches and children sleeping on dirty and filthy mattresses with holes in their clothing. There isn't anything that would surprise me."

"We don't need to take your car, lets walk," said Teach, "It's only a few blocks away." With that, they commenced walking, hand in hand. As they walked over the Causeway, Debra asked "Now where are you taking me?"

"We're almost there," replied Teach, "We have to walk around here, and under the bridge." "You live under the bridge!" "You seem surprised," said Teach, "you said nothing surprises you."

Preach, Amos, No Brains, One Lip, Ebenezer and several others appeared in the light of several bonfires. Clearly visible was Al Capone in his cage.

"We're getting married!" announced Teach, "I'm here to get my things!" "Congratulations, congratulations went the men as they hugged and shook hands.

Debra looked at Teach, "So you live under the bridge with these men, and a rooster!" "She be my egg layin bird," went Amos, "the finest egg layin bird I ever had."

They all laughed.

Chapter Forty-nine:

THE HEARING

Courthouse Square is a two-block area in Downtown Miami that contains the federal courts. The old federal courthouse was finished in 1933, it is a classic Mediterranean Revival Structure. The fresco painted ceilings and carved wood were from a period in which opulence was the operative phrase.

Although the building had largely remained unused since 2008, it housed a large main courtroom whose wood work and painted frescoes were something from another time, another place.

In order to house the large crowd which was expected that day, Chief Judge William McBain decided to reopen the main courtroom, closed the year before, one last time.

"Here Ye Here Ye, the Court of the United States of America, Honorable William McBain presiding, is now in session, all rise."

The Judge entered and took his seat. "Everyone may now be seated," said the Marshal.

"We call the case of Richard Bradford versus the United States of America. Are all parties present?"

"With that, Mr. Hooper stood up. "The Plaintiff is ready your honor."

"And how about the government?"

The United States Assistant Attorney stood up with the words, "The United States Government is also ready, Your Honor." "There he is," thought Teach, "the man responsible for putting me away."

"Thank you, Mr. Hooper and Mr. Ratley," said the judge, "I'd like to take care of a preliminary issue."

"The Plaintiff in this matter, Mr. Bradford, who was the defendant in the underlying criminal case, has filed a motion to vacate his sentence under 28 United States Code Section 2255, a "'habeas'" action, is that correct Mr. Hooper.?"

"Yes," he replied.

"In order to proceed with an action under 28 United States Code Section 2255, it is my understanding that the law requires that a defendant must be 'in custody.' In order to satisfy this requirement, he must either be in prison or jail or have his or her liberty under some form of restraint."

The United States Attorney rose. "Your honor, the Government concedes that issue. The defendant is presently under supervised release pursuant to the original judgment in this case."

"Is that correct, Mr. Hooper?" asked the court. "Yes, Your Honor, we believe that to be the case.

"When is supervised release scheduled to terminate?" asked the court. Mr. Ratley responded, "I have the probation officer here in the courtroom. Based upon his understanding, supervised release is scheduled to terminate tomorrow."

"Okay then, let's proceed" said the court, "Plaintiff call your first witness."

"Your honor," replied Mr. Hooper, "Plaintiff calls Dr. Ralph Hutchinson."

"Swear in the witness," the Judge announced to the court clerk.

"Place your hand on the bible. Do you swear to tell the truth, the whole truth and nothing but the truth?"

"I do."

"Dr. Hutchinson," please state your occupation."

"I am director of forensic science for the F.B.I. crime lab in Louisville

Kentucky."

"How long have you held that job?"

"Two years."

"And how is it that you came to find that the position you sought was available?"

"Objection, your honor, not relevant," belched the United States Attorney.

"Objection overruled," responded the court, "answer the question."

"The former director is under indictment, and I was asked to take over supervision of the crime lab based upon my education, qualifications, and my thirty years previous experience as a forensic analyst."

"Tell me about your education and experience," asked Mr. Hooper

"I have a BA degree in biochemistry from The University of California, a masters and P.H.D. from Harvard University. I have been involved in the arena of forensic science for more than thirty years. I have also authored seven publications on the subject, including three on the science of identification through DNA analysis."

"What is DNA analysis, Doctor?"

"DNA, is short for deoxyribonucleic acid. It is the material that makes up the genetic code of almost all living organisms. It can be found in hair, blood, and semen and if matched properly can tell the specific individual from whom the sample came from with mathematical certainty."

"What do you mean by 'mathematical certainty?'"

"By that, I mean within several billions."

"Now when you were appointed to take over operations at the Kentucky lab, did you do an evaluation of methods and procedure used by that particular facility as far as past analysis is concerned?"

"I did."

"And what did you find?"

"I found that trained monkeys could have done a better job."

"Objection!" screamed the United States Attorney.

"Objection overruled," said the court, "I'm interested in hearing what he has to say."

"Can you elucidate?" asked the defense counsel."

"Well," there are eight identified problems with the collection and examination of DNA evidence in forensic matters, and they are:

One: Proper taking of a sample

Two: Proper labeling of a sample.

Three: Proper storage and transportation of a of sample

Four: Proper testing of samples.

Five: Proper communication with others such as placing results in DNA data bases and dissemination to others of the results so that other databases can be checked for matches as well.

Six: Unqualified employees hired to do the testing.

Seven: Overworked employees, doing the testing on a deadline.

Eight: Dishonest employees hired to do the testing."

"And did you find any of these problems in this particular case?"

"All eight."

There was a gasp from the audience.

"We will adjourn this matter for lunch," announced the court, "I'll see you back here at 1:30 p.m."

Chapter Fifty:
It Gets Worse

"Tell me how samples are received and processed."

"Well, the way we receive samples is from various law enforcement agencies across the country. When the samples are received, they are supposed to be sealed. The first thing that we do is verify that the sample is in fact sealed, and if it is not, we reject it."

"Was this sample you received from the Brunswick Georgia Incarceration Facility sealed?"

"That's a good question. It came in a plastic zip lock bag that had tape over the opening. But the tape had either been tampered with, or the adhesive had somehow melted in the heat."

"Melted in the heat?"

"My understanding is that the tape was coming off, and that there was a question as to whether the sample was acceptable or not?"

"Aren't samples that contain DNA supposed to be kept at a specific temperature?"

"The samples are optimally supposed to be stored at minus 112 degrees. Certainly, no warmer than minus four degrees.

"So, Doctor, let me get this straight," asked Mr. Hooper, "The tape on the sample had melted in the heat?"

"That's correct," responded Dr. Hutchinson,"

"In simple terms, what does that mean?"

"What it means is that the sample is now degraded and unusable for testing purposes.

"But the record reflects that a test was in fact done?"

"Yes," was the response, "a dry test."

"What is a 'dry test.'"

"A 'dry test' is really not a test at all. It is where the analyst claimed to do a test, but never in fact did one at all."

"Well, then, where do results come from in this 'dry test?'"

"They were faked."

"They were faked?"

"That is what the worker confessed to doing."

"Objection," belched the United States Attorney.

Sustained, ruled the court.

"Tell me what it was that you found, without telling me about what the worker told you."

"What I found was that the sample had never been tested, that in fact that it was untestable as received."

"So, the result was not supported by factual evidence?"

"Correct."

"What qualifications does one have to have to be a forensic analyst?"

"A high school degree."

"Is that all?"

"Yes."

"By the way, did you retest the victim's sample in preparation for this hearing?"

"I did."

"And did you find semen?"

"Yes."

"And did you compare it to a newly provided and properly submitted sample which contained Mr. Bradford's DNA?"

"I did."

"And did this semen, which was originally obtained from the victim, match the DNA of the newly provided sample from Mr. Bradford?"

"No, it did not."

Another gasp emanated from the crowd and tears came down Debra's face.

"Quiet in the courtroom," demanded the bailiff.

"Who did the semen in the victim's sample come from?"

"Objection your honor!"

"Sustained."

"Your witness," said the Judge to the Assistant United States Attorney

"Dr. Hutchinson, you weren't there when the original testing was done, were you?"

"No."

"So how do you know what happened."

"After finding irregularities, the crime lab technician was confronted. She admitted what she did and that it was 'worse than not telling the truth.'"

"Objection move to strike answer," said the United States Attorney

"You opened the door," said the judge.

"I have no further questions," responded Mr. Ratley

"Is the plaintiff ready to call its next witness?" asked the court

"We are, your honor,

The plaintiff calls Jezebel Freiden."

"Swear in the witness," commanded the court.

"Place you hand on the bible. Do you swear to tell the truth, the whole truth and nothing but the truth?"

"I do."

"Please state your name," asked Mr. Hooper.

"Jezebel Freiden."

"Please tell me what you do? Ms. Freiden."

"Presently I am unemployed, but I used to be an analyst for the FBI Crime lab in Kentucky."

"Can you tell me the circumstances upon which you left your employment?"

"I was fired for contriving false results for DNA tests and for lying in court and in court related proceedings."

"Were you involved in the case of United States of America versus Richard Bradford?"

"I was."

"What was your involvement in the case?"

"I was the one responsible for conducting the forensic analysis of the DNA samples taken in that matter."

"Was there something that happened that was out of the ordinary?"

"Yes, Mr. Bradford's sample fell to the floor and broke open."

"When it fell to the floor, was it still usable?"

"No," it had become contaminated, and before we even realized what had happened, everything had been swept up and thrown in the trash."

She hung her head.

"They work us too hard, they don't pay us enough, and they demand results. I needed a job so I had to do something, I had to do something."

"So, what is it that you did?" asked the Mr. Hooper.

"I divided up the sample that came from the victim and I placed Mr. Bradford's name on it."

"So, in other words, the Plaintiff Richard Bradford's name was placed on a sample of the same genetic material that was retrieved from the victim, thus creating an exact match."

"Yes."

"Why didn't you tell anyone?"

"Because I was scared, I have kids, and was afraid that I might lose my job."

"It's getting late in the day," stated the court, "We'll reconvene tomorrow at 8:00 a.m. sharp."

"She was afraid of losing her job," Teach looked to his attorney, "afraid of losing her job."

Chapter Fifty-one:

Day Two

"How many witnesses are you going to call today," asked the judge.
"I have one witness, possibly two," replied Mr. Bradford's attorney.
"Call your first witness."
"Plaintiff calls Melenia Aberdeen to the stand."

Teach looked back at Debra, then turned around to see the girl, now a woman, who had been his accuser. Bleach blond, skinny to the point of emaciation, and face lined with age that told a story far older than her years, she was dressed in orange and white striped prison issue clothing. A guard who escorted her to the stand sat nearby.

"Clerk, please swear in the witness."
"Place your right hand on the bible. Do you swear to tell the truth, the whole truth and nothing but the truth?"
"I do," she responded.
"Please have a seat in the witness chair," said the court.
"Your witness, Mr. Hooper."
"Please state your name for the record."
"Melenia Aberdeen."
"Where do you presently reside, Ms. Aberdeen?"

"I presently reside at the women's unit of the Lowell Correctional facility in Marion County, Florida.

"Why are you presently incarcerated?"

"Objection,"

"Goes to credibility of witness," responded Hooper.

"Overruled, answer the question," ordered the judge.

"I am serving a three-year sentence for prostitution."

"Is that all," asked Teach's Counsel.

"No, they also accused me of robbing a man who was one of my customers, of putting some kind of drug his drink, stealing his wallet and his gold watch."

"Is that the only crime that you've been convicted of?"

"No, I've been arrested a few times."

"A few?" and Mr. Hooper let drop to the floor a list of what appeared to be page after page of arrest records.

"By a '"few',"' do you mean ten, twenty, thirty, maybe one hundred times?"

"Objection,"

"Overruled, answer the question."

"Yes," she responded as she hung her head and cried, "but I've changed."

"Do you know the plaintiff, Richard Bradford."

"I do, he was my Eighth-grade science teacher."

"Is there another reason that you know him?"

"Yes," he's the man I lied about, the one I said 'tried to rape me.'"

"What exactly do you mean?"

"I wasn't telling the truth. I sent several letters admitting that I lied, to the United States Attorney. The first was over two years ago."

"Objection."

"Overruled."

"What kind of letters?"

"Well, while in prison I decided to clear my conscience. I could no longer live with the lie that I had told, I decided to lead a new life."

Preach looked over at Amos.

"Well, as I said in the letters I wrote to the United States Attorney, I was fourteen years old at the time of the 'rape.'"

"It wasn't really a "'rape'," was it?"

"No, Mr. Bradford chased me to get my cigarettes, we fell in the mud and struggled."

"What happened next?"

"I screamed 'rape.'"

"Why?"

"Because I was scared, I was young, I needed to get the attention off of myself."

"But you knew it was a lie?"

"Yes, I did."

"Why did you continue to insist that he raped you?"

"It's a complicated story, it has to do with my mother and my stepfather."

"How so?"

"This is hard to discuss," she broke down crying, "but my stepfather raped me."

"How many times did this occur?"

"It was a daily occurrence."

"Why didn't you tell someone?"

"I tried telling my mother, but she called me a 'whore' and a 'liar.'"

"What happened after the charges were filed against your teacher?"

"Mother was ecstatic, she talked about the money she would get by suing the school system."

"And she did get money, didn't she?"

"Yes, she settled with the county for two and a half million dollars."

"And what did you receive?"

"Five million dollars."

"There was another audible gasp from the audience."

"What happened to the money?"

"I spent it on drugs and things, a boyfriend stole the rest."

"You say your life has changed?"

"Yes, I found religion and I want to tell the truth."

"Tell me about the letters you wrote to the United States Attorney."

"I wrote them two years ago, and sent them to him."

"You mean the man sitting over there?" asked Hooper, pointing to Assistant United States Attorney Ratley."

"Yes."

"Did he ever get back to you?"

"No, I never heard anything at all."

"That's all I have."

"Your witness, Mr. Ratley"

"Ma'am, you were traumatized after the event, weren't you?"

"Objection, what event is he referring to?"

"After the rape," replied Ratley.

"There was no rape," responded the witness, "not by him, but I was scared and did what my mother told me to do."

"You had psychological trauma after the event, didn't you?"

"Yes, I saw doctors."

"And you never told those doctors about the relationship you had with your stepfather, did you?"

"Objection."

"Overruled."

"No."

"So, were you lying then, or are you lying now?"

"I'm telling the truth, I wrote to tell you, but you wouldn't listen."

"That's all I have," said the Government Attorney

"Redirect?" asked the court.

"Is this one of the letters?" asked Mr. Hooper

"Yes."

"Can you please read it to the court."

The Cockfight

"Dear United States Attorney Ratley, I am writing this letter to correct a grave injustice. I lied about the teacher who I accused of raping me. I was young and under a lot of pressure and cannot sleep with this grave injustice on my conscience. Please understand that I am sorry for what I did."

"Did you receive a response to that letter?"

"No."

"What did you do next?"

"I sent him another letter saying the same thing."

"Did you receive a response to that letter?"

"No."

"Plaintiff rests its case."

"Does the Government have any witnesses?"

"The Government calls Billy Bob Hiram to the stand."

"Do you swear to tell the truth, the whole truth and nothing but the truth," asked the clerk to the large man with his hand on the bible."

"I do."

"Please state your name for the record," asked Assistant United States Attorney Ratley."

"Billy Bob Hiram.

"Where do you live, Mr. Hiram?"

"I live in Brunswick Georgia."

"They call me "'Septic Man,'" I clean septic tanks in South Georgia and North Florida."

"Do you remember an event that occurred on December 22nd, 1995?"

"I'll never forget it."

"Tell me what you remember?"

"Well, me and Bubba Thornton had been out huntin coons. We stopped at the roadside service station in Brunswick to take a leak and get some Ho Ho's from the snack machine, that's when I saw a man chasin this young thing through the woods."

"'Something ain't right,' I says to Bubba, then I hear the girl scream."

"What did you hear her scream?" asked Ratley.

"'Rape!' It was clear as day."

"What happened next?"

"I goes running and calls for Bubba. They was rollin in the mud and he was grabbing at her clothing, me and Bubba subdued him," he chuckled.

"Are you sure you heard the word 'rape.'"

"It was plain as day."

"No more questions."

"Your witness," said the court.

"Good morning Mr. Hiram, I'm Robert Hooper and I represent Mr. Bradford."

"Someone got to represent everyone," answered Billy Bob.

"That's right," replied Mr. Hooper, "you seem like a pretty smart man."

"They call me a 'Septic Genius.'"

"Now what do you mean by 'grabbling at her clothing?'"

"Well, he was definitely grabbing at something."

"Did you see a pack of cigarettes in the young girl's hand?"

"You think I'm stupid, why would he grab her cigarettes when he can buy a pack for himself at the J & J liquor stop."

"I'm going to show you this pack of cigarettes."

"Please mark it as defense exhibit B," Hooper asked the clerk.

"Can you tell me if you recognize it?"

"Of course, I do, it's a pack of Camel cigarettes, same brand that my own fourteen-year-old daughter smokes."

"Tell me about your friend Bubba, where is he?"

"Bubba's gone to the great beyond."

"How did your friend die?"

"They say that he was driving the wrong way on a four-lane highway, that he was 'drunk' or something like that."

"Blood alcohol level of .32?" asked Hooper

"Objection."

"Overruled," said the court, "answer the question if you know it?"

"I just know that they said he was 'drunk.'"

"He was your drinking buddy, wasn't he?"

"We were friends."

"Did you and him have any drinks before you hit the rest stop that day in 1995?"

"We only had a couple of beers, we weren't drunk."

"I have no further questions."

"Redirect?" asked the court.

"No, the Government rests," responded Mr. Ratley.

"Any rebuttal witnesses?"

"The plaintiff calls Richard Bradford to the stand."

"Do you swear to tell the truth, the whole truth and nothing but the truth," asked the clerk, Bradford's hand on the bible.

"Yes."

"Please state your name for the record," asked his counsel.

"Richard Bradford."

"Where do you reside?"

"Until last Sunday, under the MacArthur Causeway in Miami, Florida."

"Where do you reside now?"

"With my fiancé Debra McMillan in her apartment."

"At one time, you had a different life, didn't you?"

"I did."

"How so?"

"I was married and had two kids, I was employed as a math and science teacher with the Dade County School System."

"Were you a good teacher?"

"I was teacher of the year in 1994."

"What changed?"

"I went on a field trip with a class of eighth grade students. I was the only supervising teacher on the bus we were on, the other teacher was too sick to go on the trip."

"We had just passed the Georgia State line when I was approached by a student who told me that 'Melenia Aberdeen has cigarettes.'"

"Did you know Melenia?"

"I did."

"How so?"

"We had many meetings after class, discussions about her language and her improper dress."

"Did you ever have a sexual relationship with Ms. Aberdeen during those meetings?"

"No."

"Have you ever had a sexual relationship with Ms. Aberdeen?"

"No."

"Did you ever attempt to have sex with Melenia Aberdeen?"

"No."

"What happened after you were told about the cigarettes?"

"I walked over to her and I asked her 'Do you have something that you shouldn't have?'"

"She said that she didn't know what I was talking about."

"Next, I told her that I would speak to her when the bus stopped. We reached the Brunswick Georgia service station and Ms. Aberdeen pushed the doors of the bus open and ran into the woods."

"Why did you chase her?"

"The first thing that went through my mind is that 'I've got to stop her from hurting herself or being hurt by someone else.' I was the custodian in charge of protecting these kids, and I had to run after her. I ran into what turned out to be a muddy swamp, fallen tree limbs everywhere. As I got closer, I could see that she had a pack of cigarettes in her hand, I tried to grab them and we both fell to the ground."

"It was then that she screamed '"Rape'!"

"What happened next?"

"Before I knew it, there was a large man sitting on my chest and another one kicking me in the head. Ever since then, my life has never been the same. I was charged with 'rape,' They claimed that I had an ongoing relationship with that girl."

"No further questions."

"Your witness, Mr Ratley."

"You plead guilty to those charges, didn't you?"

"Yes."

"And when you plead guilty you were under oath and you swore to tell the truth, is that correct?"

"They told me that the DNA evidence proved that I was having a relationship with that girl, that I was going to go to jail for the rest of my life, and that I would never see my wife and children again."

"Move to strike as nonresponsive."

"Just answer the question," admonished the court.

"Not only did you plead guilty, you stated that you were pleading guilty because you were in fact guilty, is that correct?"

"Yes."

"Where do you live now?"

"With my fiancé Debra in her apartment."

"How about before then?"

"Under the General Douglas MacArthur Causeway."

"Where did you first live upon first being released?"

"Under the Julia Tuttle Causeway in the sex offender colony."

"And that is where you were living upon your release and where you last told your probation officer that you were residing, correct?"

"Objection, your honor?"

"Where is this leading?" asked the court.

"Your honor, he was under conditions of supervised release when he was let out of prison. Apparently, he failed to notify his probation officer of his relocation, a relocation that occurred at least twice. This bears upon his credibility as a witness."

"Objection overruled."

"You did relocate, didn't you?"

"Yes."

"Twice?"

"Yes,"

"Did you notify your probation officer?"

"No."

"No more questions."

"Any redirect?" asked the court.

"Why did you move from under the Julia Tuttle?"

"It was a dangerous place and I feared for my life. I had a pastor friend who suggested that I move to a different location, I went with him to live under the MacArthur Causeway."

"And why did you move again?"

"That just happened a few days ago when I became engaged to my girlfriend Debra. She asked that I live with her in her apartment until we get married. It isn't healthy living under the causeway, one guy we know almost died from fever."

"What about your wife and kids, do you see them?"

"She filed for divorce once I went to prison. She got a restraining order as well, and I'm prohibited from seeing her or my children. I haven't seen her in over fifteen years, this case destroyed my life."

"Plaintiff has no more witnesses," stated Mr. Hooper.

"Do both sides rest?" asked the court?

Both Hooper and Ratley answered in the affirmative.

"You have the burden of proof, Mr. Hooper, let me hear from you first."

"Your honor, a grave miscarriage of justice has occurred in the underlying case, my client was accused of acts that he did not commit. Evidence was put forth against him, damning evidence that was invented and contrived by individuals employed by the federal government."

The Cockfight

"My client's due process rights were denied. Due Process is the requirement that all legal protections accorded to an individual under the law are respected. In this particular case, evidence put forth by the government was fabricated. As a result of this fabrication, my client was placed in a position whereby he had no alternative but to plead guilty to the charges.

"His life has been destroyed through the admitted perpetration of a fraud by worker or workers at a government facility, whose sole authorization was to properly analyze evidence. What they did was contrive and invent results.

"The witness testimony in this case is compelling. Under no circumstances would the government have even had a case had the evidence been properly transported, stored and analyzed, and had the evidence not been discarded and falsely reassembled by the worker whose testimony you heard.

"In the interest of justice, Plaintiff requests that the conviction against him be thrown out and that a new trial in this matter be granted."

"Mr. Ratley," said the judge, "Let me hear from you."

"Your honor, I see no reason to overturn the conviction. The defendant plead guilty in this matter, in fact he admitted his guilt. As far as the witnesses are concerned, it's not uncommon for a victim to later feel sorry for their accuser, I can't see any reason why the court should rule in favor of Mr. Bradford.

"Mr. Hiram testified that he witnessed the assault, and it was pretty clear to him that Mr. Bradford wasn't going after any cigarettes. Sure, the lab technician admitted that she lied, but the independent evidence of Mr. Hiram, an eye witness, should be looked upon by the court as dispositive in this matter. Further, the plaintiff's credibility is in question, twice he has moved without notifying his probation officer.

"The plaintiff has not met his burden, and cannot show that his due process rights in this matter were denied. The Court should deny the Motion to Vacate Sentence in this matter and rule in favor of the Government."

"We're going to break for lunch," stated the judge, "We'll reconvene at two p.m., and I'll announce my ruling."

"So how do you think the court is going to rule," Teach asked his friends as they sat down for lunch with him.

"Oh, the Lord's with us today, I know it," responded Preach, "still, I've got a funny feeling about those questions the Ratley guy was asking."

"You be meanin them ones about relocation?" asked Amos.

"Yes," replied Preach, "they have me a little bit concerned.

"Whatever happens, I'll never abandon you," Debra turned to Teach as they held hands, "I'll never abandon the man I love, never!"

Chapter Fifty-two:

The Ruling

"All rise," ordered the bailiff as the judge entered the courtroom. "You may be seated," said the judge.

"Plaintiff has filed a Motion to Set Aside His Conviction under 28 United States Code section 2255. The law requires that the petitioner prove that the sentence imposed was in violation of the Constitution or laws of the United States, or that the court was without jurisdiction to impose such a sentence, or the sentence was in excess of the maximum authorized by law. This is the proof needed to allege a Constitutional error.

"The scope of review of non-constitutional error is more limited than that of constitutional error. A non-constitutional error does not provide a basis for collateral attack unless it involves a fundamental defect which inherently results in a complete miscarriage of justice, or is inconsistent with the rudimentary demand or requirements of procedure.

"The court has heard from the witnesses in this case and has considered all of the facts and evidence put forth by the parties.

"Key is the fact that there is an eye witness to the event. Although the victim has recanted her testimony, it is not uncommon for victims who later feel remorse to change their account of what previously happened.

"Additionally, there was a plea hearing in which the plaintiff plead guilty. At this hearing, he was under oath and was asked the following question, 'Are you pleading guilty because you are in fact guilty?'"

"Mr. Bradford answered in the affirmative."

"It is this court's finding that the plaintiff has not met his burden. A new trial in the underlying matter is hereby denied."

"Don't worry," defense counsel Hooper whispered to Teach, "I expected this. We'll be filing an appeal."

"Your Honor, may we take a short break before this matter concludes?" asked the United States Attorney.

"We'll reconvene in fifteen minutes," replied the judge.

The United States Attorney walked over to Teach's table along with the probation officer.

Chapter Fifty-three:
A Surprise

"I have something to give you," said the officer, it read "Petition For Warrant For Violation Of The Conditions Of Supervised Release."

"Failure To Report To Probation Officer As Instructed, 'A Grade C Violation.' 'Failure To Report Change In Residence,' Another 'Grade C Violation.'"

"Imprisonment should not exceed more than two years."

"Do you mean to tell me that you are charging this man with violation of conditions of supervised release, when the conviction for the crime that he was charged with was bogus from start to finish, and where you ruined this man's life on lies?" boomed Mr. Hooper.

Debra stood up and addressed the United States Attorney.

"You bastard, you degenerate bastard, you only uphold the law when it's on your side, but if it isn't you just ignore it. You know nothing about justice or human decency, your only interest is putting your own career ahead by obtaining as many convictions as you can. You're the lowest form of human trash that ever-set foot on this earth."

Preach came over to tell her to sit down.

"Don't get too close to the preacher man," replied Ratley, "We know a little bit about a murder that occurred under the Julia Tuttle."

"You don't scare me," said Preach, "I know who's on my side," he looked up.

"And we also know a little bit about some funny things going on with roosters under the bridge, as well as," and Ratley looked directly at Teach, "and something about private personal information that came from a computer traced to your girlfriend."

"All rise," ordered the Marshall as the judge re-entered the courtroom.

"Your honor," said the United States Attorney, "The government has charged the defendant with violating his conditions of supervised release."

"Well then," replied the judge, "Why don't we address that issue with regards to pre-trial release."

"Your witness"

"The government calls probation officer Jack Riley."

"Please state your name for the record," asked the United States Attorney.

"Jack Riley, United States Probation Officer."

"And were you assigned to supervise Richard Bradford?"

"I was, but he disappeared."

"Did you have any contact with him?"

"No, no contact whatsoever, we had no idea where he was living."

"Your witness Mr. Hooper," went the court.

"Mr. Riley, how long have you been a federal probation officer?"

"Twenty-three years."

"And during the time you've been a probation officer have you any experience with placement of so called 'sex offenders' under the Julia Tuttle Causeway?"

"I have, sex offenders have been living there for several years, and officially we began placement under this bridge when the law in Miami-Dade County Florida changed."

"How So?"

"Well, a law was passed prohibiting individuals who were convicted of sex related offenses from living within two thousand five hundred feet of schools, parks, bus benches and other places where children and families gather."

"What effect did the law have?"

"Well, the only place that met that description was under the Julia Tuttle Causeway."

"Tell me about living conditions under the Causeway, were there four walls and a roof? Bathroom and shower facilities?"

"No, the residents lived under a bridge that only provided shelter on one side and from above. There weren't any bath or shower facilities either."

"So that when the wind and rain came, they were pummeled, and with no sanitation they basically defecated into the bay and took their baths in that same bay?"

"That is correct."

"Was it safe living under this bridge, I mean with regards to the individuals one would associate with?"

"Objection,"

"Overruled, answer the question."

"Well, I'm not sure how to answer that."

"I have here a printout of from the Miami Dade County Police," Hooper walked over to Ratley and gave him a copy.

"It says here that over the last year, the police have been called to this colony 'five hundred and six times' for various complaints ranging from 'sexual assault to murder.'" "Are you aware of this?"

"Well, if it says so, I'm not in a position to contradict it."

"No more questions."

"No redirect, the government calls Jaime Colona."

Preach, Amos, No Brains and One Lip looked at each other. "It's Rollie," blurted Amos, "I told you they's something strange about that boy."

"Quiet in the courtroom," ordered the Marshall.

"Please state your name for the record," asked Ratley.

"Officer Jaime Colona of the Miami-Dade County Police."

"Were you assigned to a specific detail?"

"Yes, I was with the undercover unit."

"Have you ever encountered Mr. Bradford?"

"Yes, under the MacArthur Causeway, he was there with other individuals."

"Do you see any of those other individuals in the courtroom?"

"Yes," he pointed to Preach, Amos, One Lip and No Brains.

"So, in other words," asked Mr. Ratley, "he was living under the MacArthur Causeway and not the Julia Tuttle?"

"Correct."

"Was there something else you noticed?"

"Yes, they had a bird in cage under the bridge."

"Do you know what it was for?"

"Well, the man in the wheelchair back there," he pointed to Amos, "said that it was his 'egg-layin bird.'"

"Did that make you suspicious?"

"Well, I did some research and found out that it was a rooster."

"What else did you find?" asked the United States Attorney?

"I did some more research and found out that roosters don't lay eggs."

Hooper looked at Teach, "Is he really that stupid?"

What do you think they were really doing with the rooster?"

"Objection," screamed Hooper

"What is this all about?" asked the judge

"Well, your honor," replied Ratley, "my understanding is that there were rooster fights occurring under the bridge."

"What does this base speculation have to do with anything?" Teach's counsel responded.

"Objection sustained," stated the judge.

"The government has no more questions."

"Mr. Bradford calls Debra McMillan," announced Hooper

"Please state your name."

"Debra McMillan."

"Where do you reside?" Hooper continued

"In my apartment on 103rd street in Biscayne Park, Dade County, Florida."

"Does anyone reside there with you?"

"Yes, my fiancé, Richard Bradford."

"How long have you been engaged?"

"For two weeks."

"When do you plan upon getting married?

She looked at Richard with longing eyes, "I hope as soon as possible."

"What do you do for a living, Ms. McMillan?"

"I am a licensed social worker for the State of Florida."

"Have you ever been convicted of a crime?"

"No"

"Do you agree to be custodian for Mr. Bradford and insure that he will obey all conditions of pre-trial release, that he will appear at trial, not flee the jurisdiction and not violate the law?"

"I do."

"No more questions," said Hooper

"Your witness, Mr Ratley."

"Good afternoon Ms. McMillan, who did you say you work for?"

"The Florida Department of Social Services, as a social worker."

"In that capacity, do you take and keep personal information from clients?"

"Objection, relevance."

"What's the relevance?" asked the court

"Well," said Mr. Ratley, "We have learned that sensitive personal information taken by Ms. McMillan has been released to the public. We question her honesty and this bears upon whether or not she would not be a proper custodian."

"Overruled, answer the question."

"I had a computer that was stolen, I guess they got some information that was on it."

"Did you report the theft?"

"Objection," loudly announced Hooper

"Sustained," ruled the court.

"I have no further questions," said Ratley.

"Argument?" asked the court, "Government goes first."

"It is the government's position that if you release this man, there is a strong likelihood that you will never see him again. Further, I'm not sure what he was doing under the bridge with his friends, but I'm suspicious that he may be involved in some sort of cockfighting ring."

"Lastly, his fiancé, cannot be trusted. She mishandled personal information that somehow made its way to the public."

"Mr. Bradford is a flight risk and is a danger to the community, he should not be released."

"Defense Counsel?"

"Your honor, the evidence against my client is tenuous at best, non-existent at worst. He is the victim in this case, nothing less, a teacher who lost his job, his family and his freedom on lies and fabrications. There is no reason for him to flee, he himself came forward to clear his record.

"Lastly, this attempt to accuse him of being involved in a rooster fighting ring is outrageous, and the attempt to impugn the integrity of his fiancé is beyond words.

"He left the Julia Tuttle because of the dangerous conditions there, not to mention the lack of shelter. Murders, sexual assaults, all type of mayhem, day in and day out. He was once the Teacher of The Year of Miami-Dade County. This court should consider that fact as well as the fact that there is substantial evidence pointing to his innocence. Although the Court ruled against him, we will be filing an appeal. That is all."

"Here is my ruling," said the Judge, "It is clear from the record that the defendant is a risk of flight. He has ignored previous orders of the court, and relocated on at least two separate occasions without notifying his probation officer. He was charged and convicted of a serious crime, thus, he is a danger to the community. The Defendant's motion for pre-trial release is hereby denied."

Debra broke down in tears as the Marshals took Richard Bradford into custody.

"Where will they be taking him, where will they be taking him?" she cried, tears streaming down her face.

"He'll be in federal lockup downtown until the hearing," responded Hooper, "that should occur in approximately thirty days. Meanwhile, I'll be working on the appeal."

Preach uncharacteristically lost his temper, "These hypocrites who work for the government and their so-called 'justice system.' They live in a society where they demand strict adherence to the law, but only when the law is on their side. When the law isn't on their side, they simply ignore it. Yet I know that come a day, they will reap what they shall sow, they will reap what they shall sow," he spoke with great determination, his right fist clenched as he looked up to the sky.

When the group of bridge dwellers left the courtroom and wondered into the hallway, only sadness remained. "If that don't beat all," lamented Amos, "if that don't beat all, I never thought that the system could do that to a white man."

"White, black, Hispanic or Anglo, it's an unfair and unjust system in an unjust world." That's why I became an attorney," said Mr. Hooper, "thinking that I could make a difference."

"You can make a difference," Preach put his hand on the dejected attorney's shoulders, "You've just got to keep up the faith, you can't lose faith."

"You know," replied Amos, "I be thinkin that it ain't over till it's over."
"Why that's the spirit," responded Preach.

"You can't let the bastards grind you down," Amos continued. "Seems I've heard that phrase somewhere before," responded Preach.

Attorney Hooper, left the courthouse. He went back to his office and commenced the hard work he believed necessary to overturn the Court's decision, work that was just beginning.

Chapter Fifty-four:
The Most Hated Inmates

Child Molesters are by far the most hated individuals in jails and prisons across the country. In order to protect them from the other inmates, who consider harming or killing them as a favor to the community, many are placed in "protective custody," also known as "solitary confinement."

Teach found himself in 'protective custody' at a federal lockup in Western Miami-Dade County, as his appeal moved forward.

Having limited contact with others, Debra's frequent visits helped to lift his spirits.

"You know everything is riding on the appeal," said Teach.

"I know that Mr. Hooper is working hard, very hard to get you out," responded Debra, "But this system, this whole sorry and ungodly system is working hard to stop the truth from coming out."

"I know this sounds strange, but you know who I'm worried about?" responded Teach.

"Who's that?" responded Debra.

"Melenia."

"Melenia?" why her.

"Well maybe it's the teacher still inside of me, but I get the feeling that she's got a very fragile personality. If the court grants the appeal, that will mean a new trial and I wonder how she would handle that, or if Assistant United States Attorney Ratley even cares."

"He doesn't give a hoot or a holler," responded Debra, "Preach said it all."

"Preach?" "What did Preach Say?"

"He said that they're 'hypocrites who only believe in the law when it's on their side, otherwise they ignore it. But there will come a day when they will reap what they sow, they will reap what they sow.'"

"Preach said that! I'd love to have heard him."

"He's going be visiting you. Just him, because the other guys don't have necessary identification."

"Well, I look forward to seeing him, and I look forward to getting out so that we can get married."

Both of them started crying.

Next day Preach appeared, "So how's the Teacher of the Year doing?" "I'm doing okay, as can be expected. You know I met with my attorney and he said that 'everything's on hold pending the appeal.'"

"How long does he expect it to take?" "Well, even with an expedited appeal, it might take as long as a year on more. But he feels that in either case, I'll have served whatever time the judge would have given me for violation of my supervised release conditions."

"You mean for the supervised release you never would have been on had the justice system worked and an innocent man not been convicted."

"You know Preach, I still feel that I did the right thing by fighting to clear my name. In the end, someway, somehow, I can't stop believing that justice will prevail."

"We can only pray about that," replied Preach, there's a lot of lost souls out there, not the least being that Ratley guy. I even pray for his soul, to save it from eternal Hell and Damnation."

"How's Al Capone, how is he doing?" "Al hasn't been the same since you left, but we're all keeping a good eye on him and making sure he's well fed and cared for."

"Make sure that El Cabron guy doesn't get too close."

"You know I will, you know I will"

"And please look after Debra, she comes to visit me every visitation day but I know she's sad."

"I'll try and keep her spirits up."

Chapter Fifty-five:

The Decision

Tears streamed down Debra's face as she sat next to Attorney Hooper, both having traveled to the jail to read the decision handed down by the Eleventh Circuit Court of Appeal.

"It is the decision of this court that Mr. Richard Bradford has met his burden of proof and his request for a new trial is hereby granted."

"What does this mean," responded Teach, "does this mean that I'm innocent, free to go?"

"What it means is that you've been granted a new trial. What that means is that you will have the right to call witnesses and confront your accuser."

"What if the jury finds me guilty?"

"They won't find you guilty," replied Debra "With the confession of Melenia that she lied, along with the admission of fraud that the lady from the crime lab admitted to, there's nothing that they have against you."

"We're going to be going before the judge on a motion for pre-trial release in two weeks. I'm going to move that Debra be your custodian."

"I want to thank you Mr. Hooper for all that you've done for me, thank you for all of your hard work and effort."

Two weeks later the courtroom was crowded with Teaches friends, Preach,

Amos, One Lip, and No Brains were there. One lip scowled at Ratley, but it was hard to tell, as his mouth always appeared to be in a similar scowling position.

"This Court is now in session, All Rise!" ordered the Marshall.

"Mr. Ratley," said the judge, "Is it the government's intention to proceed with the case?"

"Yes, your honor, the government believes that it has a strong case against Mr. Bradford."

"Then let's readdress the issue of pre-trial release."

"Mr. Hooper, is it still your client's intention to marry Ms. McMillan and reside with her?"

Teach looked back at her from the defense table and she at him.

"Yes, your honor, it is my understanding."

"What is the position of the government, Mr. Ratley?"

"It is the government's position that Mr. Bradford is a dangerous sex offender who assaulted a young girl, a student in his charge. Further, that he violated previous conditions of supervised release by relocating on at least two separate occasions without contact or communication with his probation officer.

"The government believes that he is a danger to the community and that there is a risk of flight."

"Any response from the defendant?"

"Your honor, my client has already spent a total of over eleven years in jail for a crime he has never committed and he is anxious to clear his name. He voluntarily came forward and filed his motion for a new trial, knowing that that very act would alert the government to his presence. As a result of his attempt to clear his name, he has now been incarcerated for the last year, waiting for a decision from the Court of Appeal.

"That decision has now come down from the Eleventh Circuit Court of Appeal and he has been granted a new trial, there is no reason to believe that all of the time and effort expended to clear his name that he would now flee the jurisdiction or commit a criminal offense."

"Here is my ruling," replied the Court,

"Pre-trial release is granted under the following conditions: He shall be released to the custody of his fiancé, Ms. McMillan, under the condition that within one week a valid marriage certificate shall be provided to the court and proof provided that they are married."

"This matter will be set for trial in two months."

"Court is adjourned."

Outside of the courtroom was bedlam.

"Teach be getting married Teach be getting married!" screamed Amos.

"I don't know how to thank you Mr. Hooper," said Teach.

"Don't thank me yet, unless the government dismisses these bogus charges, you're going to be in trial."

"Before that, we've got a wedding to go to," replied Preach, "Isn't this exciting."

Chapter Fifty-six:

THE GIFT

Back under the bridge, things were in a jolly mood. "We gonna have a wedding," said Amos, "We gonna have a wedding." Amos looked down from his wheelchair at Al Capone, and spoke the words again, "We gonna have a wedding."

Al Capone let out a "cluck."

"Isn't it exciting," replied Preach.

"It sure is," responded Amos, "What we be getting Teach and Debra for a gift?"

"That's a good question," said Preach, and he pulled his out the white linings of his empty pockets.

"I be short on money too, but I be having an idea. Ebenezer and me be heading out to the street to collect some funds for a nice gift."

"How do you feel, Ebenezer?" asked Preach, "do you feel that you can do the job as Amos's wheelchair man?"

"I feel great," was the response, "It is an honor and a pleasure to be this man's wheelchair captain, especially after what you guys did for me."

"Hey," replied Amos, "you just be remembering that I be the captain, you be the pusher man."

"Where are you going to be heading?" asked Preach. "We be goin where the spressway off ramp be."

"You be careful," warned Preach, "there's a lot of traffic over there."

"That be where the money be," Amos replied, and off they went, Amos, pushed by Ebenezer, out to raise money to buy a gift for their friends Teach and Debra.

Approximately twenty minutes later, Debra and Teach appeared. "We drove over and parked as close as we could get," went Teach, "Where's Amos?"

"Oh, he's out with Ebenezer," went Preach, "just taking in the sun."

Teach leaned down to Al's cage. "How are you doing little fellow?" At the same time, Capone let out a "cluck."

"You're a pretty bird, aren't you," said Debra as she spoke to the bird, "do you have any eggs for us today?"

Teach and Preach both laughed.

"You know," went Teach, "I've been thinking." "What have you been thinking about?" Preach asked, in a knowing way.

"I've been thinking that Al would be happy on a farm somewhere, rather than cooped up in a cage under a loud and dirty expressway. Debra has found an animal rescue organization that takes in abandoned and at-risk roosters."

The horn of a loud truck could be heard, as well as the continuous "varumpt," "varumpt," "varumpt,' noise as vehicles traveled overhead.

"That's a good idea," said Preach, "but we're going to have to run it by Amos, he has a say in it as well."

"Where did you say he went?" asked Teach. "Well, I wasn't supposed to say it, but Ebenezer and him are out raising money for a wedding gift."

"How sweet," replied Debra, "raising money for a gift for us."

"Did he say he where he was going?" asked Teach

"He said he's going to the expressway off ramp," was the response. "That's a little dangerous," said Teach, a look of concern on his face, "Maybe we ought to go out looking for him."

Just as he finished his sentence, Ebenezer appeared at the entrance to the bridge, out of breath, with a look of terror on his face.

"Amos has been hit! Amos been hit!" Ebenezer cried.

No one saw the truck as it barreled down the overpass, going far too fast and driving far too erratically. The driver hit Amo's wheelchair squarely in the middle, crushing him and the chair under the wheels of the truck.

The driver fled. "Most likely had no driver's license," was the conclusion of the police officers at the scene. If he did have one, that would be the exception for Miami drivers.

"I tried to help him," lamented Ebenezer, "me and the boys tried to pull him out from under the truck, but it was no use."

"Did he have any dying words?" asked Teach.

"He said to tell you guys 'I love you,' and to 'make sure that Al Capone is taken care of.'"

Chapter Fifty-seven:
The Equation of Injustice

"You know," observed Preach, "I think that it's time to take Al to a new home. Here he is, living in a cage under an expressway. He never did nothing to no-one, but everyone tried to take advantage of him. They caged him up, deprived him of his freedom, they made him mean, angry, distrusting of others of his kind. Lastly, they devised a system where they could make money from the whole unholy process."

"You mean like the system they devised to take away my freedom," replied Teach, "and the system that captured Flathead and wouldn't let him go until he took his own life. The very same system that put Amos in a wheelchair and reduced him to begging for money on the streets of Miami, until it cost him his own life?"

Preach looked on and smiled as Debra held Teaches arm tightly.

"Keeping this bird in a cage and making him fight to the death is the same kind of injustice that they perpetrated on me and all the others. I'm just a simple math and science teacher but I know equations, an equation is a mathematical formula that stands for the fact two things are equal. It's all about the equation and this is all about injustice."

"It is the equation of injustice."

"Now you've got it," replied Preach, "Now you've got it," and he put his arm around Teach's shoulder and hugged him.

"Hadn't we better pack up Capone and head off to the animal rescue folks?" asked Teach.

"I think that's a good idea," answered Preach. "Me too," replied Debra, and the car sped off, Teach in the front seat and Preach in the back next to Al Capone's cage.

They walked into the building, situated at a farm in the Redlands. All kinds of animals could be seen, a three-legged goat, a young bear, raccoons, cats, chickens, an owl in a cage, and a german shepherd, gladly wagging his tail as he barked.

"Don't mind Rufus," said the lady, "he's blind but he's still pretty well spirited." Debra petted his head, "What a nice dog, what a nice dog."

"We've got a bird here," announced Preach, "and we believe he's at risk of being used in a cockfight!"

"That's right," said Teach, "and we're hoping that you can find a good home for him."

"What a pretty bird," replied the lady, "I think we can find a place for him."

"Goodbye," said Teach to Al, "You're a great rooster, and meeting you has really meant a lot to us."

"That it has," replied Preach.

"You taught us all about love, about loyalty, and about truth," continued Teach, "but most of all, you taught us about the meaning of injustice."

"That must be quite a bird," said the lady behind the counter. "He certainly is," replied Teach, "he certainly is."

"Does he have a name?" asked the lady.

"Al, Al Capone is his name."

Chapter Fifty-eight:
News From The Government

"I got a call from attorney Hooper," said Debra to Teach, "He wants us to come to his office as soon as we can."

"What do you think it could mean?" asked Teach.

"I don't know," replied Debra, "but he said it was important. I have to be at work today, because the Christian House of Charity is looking for a new administrator, they want me to help them with the selection process."

"I'll try to leave early to pick you up around 12:30, so we can meet the lawyer around 1:00 p.m., this is an important position that they're looking to fill and they need my input."

At twelve thirty, Debra came home to pick up Teach. "Are you washed and ready?" she asked, "and Teach appeared from the bathroom and buttoned his shirt."

"Did they find someone to fill the new administrative position?" asked Teach. "Not yet," responded Debra, "it's hard to find anyone with the right qualifications."

They sped off for the appointment with the attorney.

"Have a seat," said Mr. Hooper with a serious look on his face, "Melenia Aberdeen has committed suicide.

"Oh my God," responded Debra.

"Apparently she couldn't take the prospect of being forced to testify against you in court and so she cut her wrists."

"You know, I predicted it," replied Teach. "Anyone with a heart or a soul could see that she was in turmoil. I wonder if that rat, Ratley, gives flying f_ck about what happened to that girl, and what he put her through."

"The hell with what he put her through," loudly replied Hooper, "look what he put you through! But even this low life bastard has some kind of a moral compass, he realizes that he can't go ahead without his main witness. Here is a faxed letter from the office of United States Attorney."

"It is a short letter so I'll read it to you."

"Dear Mr. Hooper, this is to advise you that the Office of United States Attorney for the Southern District of The State of Florida has decided not to pursue the pending charges against Mr. Richard Bradford."

"Further, the government will no longer contest the motion filed on behalf of your client to clear his name."

A loud "whoop" went out from both Teach and Debra.

"Does that mean for the violation of supervised release is dismissed?" asked Teach as Debra grabbed his arm."

"It means all pending charges," answered Hooper.

Teach and Debra embraced. "Well, I guess then," said Teach, "that now we don't have to get married."

"If we don't," replied Debra, "you'll be in bigger trouble than any criminal charge." They embraced again.

Chapter Fifty-nine:

A Funeral and a Wedding.

"We are gathered here beside the bay here today," said Preach, "to honor the memory of our dear friend Amos. He was a man whose infectious laughter and glad spirit will be remembered by everyone he met.

"Amos was a friend to everyone on the streets of Miami, and when I mean by everyone, I mean by everyone who lived under a bridge or who begged for money on the side of the highway. He considered us his true friends, and this is evidenced by the fact that we were the only ones who came to claim his cremated remains.

"I spoke to the man at the crematorium and he gave me Amo's ashes as well as these two steel jacketed bullets that fell out of Amo's body and didn't burn up in the fire. I've written a letter to the fine folks of the Miami-Dade County Police Department, and I will read it here."

"Dear Miami-Dade County Police Department. Enclosed please find two bullets that fell out of the back of our dear late friend Amos Haveaseat. It is my understanding that these bullets came from your so-called 'Law enforcement officers.' We are hereby returning them to you, they took away his ability to walk but not his spirit, they took away his mobility but not his pride."

"We hereby commit Amo's ashes to the waters of Biscayne Bay. We know that God has accepted him into his fold, and that he looks after him, protects him, and guides him through eternity, until we meet again."

Preach looked at Teach, Teach opened the canister and spread his late friend's ashes into the water.

Not a dry eye was present.

"Now we'll proceed with a happier event," said Preach, "the wedding of our good friends Teach and Debra." Everyone gathered around, Ebenezer, One Lip, No Brains and fifty other residents of the bridge community, all in varying states of dress, some unkempt and others holding flowers, some with holes in their clothing, and others with their hair slicked back.

"Do you Richard Bradford take this woman, Debra McMillan, to be your lawfully wedded wife, from this day forth, to have and to hold, for better or for worse, for richer or poorer, as long as you both shall live?"

"I do."

"And do you Debra McMillan take Richard Bradford to be your lawfully wedded husband from this day forth, to have and to hold, for better or for worse, for richer or poorer, as long as you both shall live?"

"I do."

"Ring Bearer?" called out Ebenezer, "and immediately No Brains came forth, with a ring on a small pillow. He smiled, now sporting very few teeth. Teach took the ring and placed it on Debra's hand.

"I now pronounce you man and wife," both embraced in a passionate kiss, as the crowd cheered and rice flew high into the air.

Chapter Sixty:

THE DADE COUNTY YOUTH & AGRICULTURAL FAIR

The little blond-haired girl ran ahead of her parents toward the bird cages, lined up on table after table under a large tent. Relief from the heat was broken only by the whirring and whining of one rotating fan, vainly attempting to circulate air.

"Slow down Amanda, if you run too fast you might fall and get hurt," went the man, as he showed concern on his face. "Oh," went the smiling woman accompanying him, "Look how excited she is, she's excited to see the animals but most of all she's excited to be with her father."

As the little girl ran, occasionally she would stop at a cage and talk to the birds, "Hello rooster." She would smile, make faces, and run toward whatever cage's occupant caught her attention.

A particular cage caught her attention, its occupant was silky brown on its neck and underside, covered by greyish feathers that proudly pointed skyward and then looped downward toward the bottom of the cage. On the top of the cage was mounted a blue ribbon.

The little girl ran back toward her parents. She grabbed her father's hand and urged him on, "Come Daddy, come see the pretty bird." "I better see what's got her so excited," said the man to his wife.

A flash of recognition and a smile broke out on the man's face as he approached.

"Well how you doing little fellow?" he asked. "Isn't the bird pretty?" asked the little girl.

"Yes, honey, that is a very pretty rooster, a very pretty rooster," said her father.

A familiar looking lady appeared from behind the counter, "Well how the heck are you doing?" she asked.

"We're doing great," replied Debra, "I'm still working for the department of social services, and my husband here is the Administrator for the Christian House of Charity."

"Well, if that don't beat all," said the woman, "You know that I have to tell you that I've been following your husband's story in the news, everyone I know has been praying for him."

"The vicious thing that our own government did to him in the name of so called 'justice,' is reprehensible. To think that we live in a country that would do that to another human being? I'm ashamed, I can honestly say that I am ashamed," she started to cry.

Richard consoled her; "A friend who I knew well wasn't an educated man, but he was smarter than I'll ever be. Even though he was paralyzed, and in a wheelchair, he was always smiling. He knew what was important, because he knew that a person is only defeated when they make you change your attitude. You are a loser then, and only then."

"You've got to be one of the bravest people I've ever met. You have a lovely wife, and look at your daughter! It's just so wonderful to see you, so fantastic," she continued, "and will you look at Al, isn't he something, First in Show."

"Yes, he is something," responded Teach, "yes he is," and with that, Al Capone let loose with a loud "Cock-A-Doodle Doo!"

THE END

ABOUT THE AUTHOR

Frank Abrams lives in Arden, North Carolina with his wife, where he is a practicing criminal defense attorney and sometime author. He has appeared on television and public radio and has an interest in both music and photography. Recently he was in the news for finding a tintype photograph of the outlaw Billy The Kid along with Pat Garrett, the man who would later kill him.

www.ingramcontent.com/pod-product-compliance
Lightning Source LLC
Chambersburg PA
CBHW070310300125
20972CB00001B/1